BEFORE HE ENVIES

BLAKE PIERCE

Blake Pierce is author of the bestselling RILEY PAGE mystery series, which includes fifteen books (and counting). Blake Pierce is also the author of the MACKENZIE WHITE mystery series, comprising thirteen books (and counting); of the AVERY BLACK mystery series, comprising six books; of the KERI LOCKE mystery series, comprising five books; of the MAKING OF RILEY PAIGE mystery series, comprising three books (and counting); of the KATE WISE mystery series, comprising four books (and counting); of the CHLOE FINE psychological suspense mystery, comprising three books (and counting); and of the JESSE HUNT psychological suspense thriller series, comprising three books (and counting).

ONCE GONE (a Riley Paige Mystery—Book #1), BEFORE HE KILLS (A Mackenzie White Mystery—Book 1), CAUSE TO KILL (An Avery Black Mystery—Book 1), A TRACE OF DEATH (A Keri Locke Mystery—Book 1), and WATCHING (The Making of Riley Paige—Book 1) are each available as a free download on Amazon!

An avid reader and lifelong fan of the mystery and thriller genres, Blake loves to hear from you, so please feel free to visit www.blakepierceauthor.com to learn more and stay in touch.

BOOKS BY BLAKE PIERCE

BEFORE HE ENVIES

(A Mackenzie White Mystery—Book 12)

BLAKE PIERCE

TABLE OF CONTENTS

CHAPTER ONE

Mackenzie took a deep breath and closed her eyes, bracing herself and trying to stop the pain. She had read so much about the whole breathing method thing and now, as Ellington rushed her to the hospital, all of it seemed to have slipped right out of her head. Maybe it was because her water had broken and she could still feel it along the leg of her pants. Or maybe it was because she had felt her first legitimate contraction about five minutes ago and she could feel another one coming on.

Mackenzie pressed against the passenger seat, watching the city pass by in a blur of darkness, sprinkling rain, and streetlights. Ellington was behind the wheel, sitting rigid and staring out the windshield like a man possessed. He laid down on the horn as they approached a red light.

"E, it's okay, you can slow down," she said.

"No, no, we're good," he said.

With her eyes still closed against Ellington's driving, she placed her hands on the large bump of her stomach, grappling with the idea that she would be a mother in the next several hours. She could feel the baby barely stirring, perhaps just as scared of Ellington's driving as she was.

I'll see you soon, she thought. It was a thought that brought more joy than worry and for that, she was grateful.

The streetlights and signs went blaring by. She stopped paying attention to them until she saw the directional signs pointing toward the hospital emergency room.

A man stood outside at the curb, waiting for them under the awning with a wheelchair, knowing they were coming. Ellington carefully brought the car to a stop and the man waved and smiled to them with the sort of lazy enthusiasm most nurses in the ER at two in the morning seemed to have.

Ellington guided her to it as if she were made of porcelain. She knew he was being overprotective and urgent because he, too, was a little scared. But more than that, he was good to her. He always had been. And he was proving now that he was going to be good to this baby, too.

"Hey, hold on, slow down," Mackenzie said as Ellington helped her into the wheelchair.

"What? What is it? What's wrong?"

She felt another contraction coming but she still managed to flash a smile at him. "I love you," she said. "That's all."

The spell he'd been under for the last eighteen minutes—between hopping out of bed to her announcement that she was going into labor to him helping her into the wheelchair—broke for a moment and he smiled back. He leaned down and kissed her softly on the mouth.

"I love you, too."

The man at the wheelchair handles looked away, a little embarrassed. When they were done, he asked, "You guys ready to have a baby?"

The contraction hit and Mackenzie cringed against it. She remembered from the reading that they would only get worse the closer the baby came to arriving. Still, she looked past it all for a moment and nodded.

Yes, she was ready to have this baby. In fact, she could hardly wait to hold it in her arms.

She had only dilated four centimeters by eight o'clock that morning. She had gotten to know the doctor and the nurses well, but when they switched shifts, Mackenzie's mood started to change. She was tired, she was hurting, and she simply didn't enjoy the idea of another doctor coming in and poking around under her gown. But Ellington, as dutiful as ever, had managed to get her OBGYN on the phone and he was doing his best to get to the hospital as soon as he could.

When Ellington came back into the room from making the call, he was frowning. She hated to see him having crashed from his high of being her protector last night, but she was also glad she was not the only one who was experiencing a mood swing.

"What is it?" she asked.

"He'll be here for the delivery, but he won't even bother coming over until you're at least at eight centimeters. Also … I was going to bring you some waffles from the cafeteria, but the nurses say you should eat light. They'll be bringing you some Jell-O and ice chips any minute now."

Mackenzie shifted in the bed and looked down at her stomach. She preferred to look there rather than the machines and monitors they had her hooked up to. As she traced the shape of her stomach, there was a knock at the door. The newer doctor came walking in, holding her charts. He looked happy and fully refreshed, coming in off of what appeared to have been a restful night's sleep.

Bastard, Mackenzie thought.

The doctor thankfully kept the conversation to a minimum as he checked her over. Mackenzie didn't pay much attention to him, honestly. She was tired, drifting off to sleep even when he put the jelly on her stomach to check the baby's progress. She drifted off into a half-sleep for a while until she heard the doctor speaking to her.

"Mrs. White?"

"Yes?" she asked, irritated that she could not get a small nap in. She had been trying to sneak them in between contractions … anything for just a bit of rest.

"Are you feeling any new discomfort?"

"Nothing other than the same pains I've had since we got here."

"Have you felt the baby moving a great deal in the last hours?"

"I don't think so. Why … is something wrong?"

"No, not *wrong*. But I believe your baby has turned. There's a very good chance that this will be a breach delivery. And I'm getting an irregular heartbeat … nothing terribly out of the ordinary, but enough to raise concerns."

Ellington was at her side at once, taking her hand. "Breach … is that risky?"

"Hardly ever," the doctor said. "Sometimes we know the baby is already breach a few weeks out from delivery. But your baby was in the correct position during the last checkup … was even perfectly positioned when you checked in last night. But he or she has turned a bit and unless something drastic changes, I don't see your kiddo getting back into the right position. Right now, it's this heartbeat that I'm concerned about."

"So what do you recommend?" Mackenzie asked.

"Well, I'd like to do a thorough check on the baby just to make sure its sudden position change has not placed it in distress—which is what the erratic heartbeat might be. If it hasn't—and there's no reason to believe it has—then we will schedule an operating room for you as soon as we can."

The idea of skipping traditional labor was appealing, sure, but adding surgery to the birth process didn't particularly sit well with her, either.

"Whatever you think is best," Mackenzie said.

"Is it safe?" Ellington asked, not even attempting to hide the tremble of fear in his voice.

"Perfectly safe," the doctor said, wiping away the excess jelly from Mackenzie's stomach. "Of course, as with any surgery, we have to mention that there is always a risk when someone's on the table. But cesarean deliveries are very common. I've personally performed more than fifty. And I believe your OBGYN is Dr. Reynolds. She's older than I am by a stretch … don't tell her I said that … and I guarantee she's done more than I have. You're in good hands. Shall I reserve a room?"

"Yes," Mackenzie said.

"Great. I'll get a room and make sure to let Dr. Reynolds know what's going on."

Mackenzie watched him leave and then looked back down to her belly. Ellington joined her, their hands interlocking over the temporary home of their child.

"That's sort of scary, huh?" Ellington asked, kissing her on the cheek. "But we'll be okay."

"Of course we will," she said with a smile. "Think of our lives and our relationship. It almost makes sense that this kid would come into this world with a bit of drama."

She meant every word of it, but even then, in one of their most vulnerable moments together, Mackenzie was hiding more fear than she cared to let on.

Kevin Thomas Ellington was born at twelve twenty p.m. He weighed seven pounds six ounces and, according to Ellington, had his father's misshapen head and red cheeks. It wasn't quite the delivery experience Mackenzie had been expecting but when she had heard his first little cries, taking in his first breaths, she didn't care. She could have given birth to him in an elevator or some abandoned building. He was alive, he was here, and that was the important thing.

Once she heard Kevin's cries, Mackenzie allowed herself to calm down. She was lightheaded and out of it from the anesthesia from the C-section procedure and felt sleep pulling at her. She was dimly aware of Ellington at her side, complete with his white operating room cap and blue gown. He kissed her forehead and was doing nothing to hide the fact that he was openly crying.

"You did amazing," he said through his tears. "You're so strong, Mac. I love you."

She opened her mouth to return the sentiment but wasn't fully sure she'd said it. She drifted off to the beautiful sounds of her still-crying son.

The next hour or so of her life was a fragmented kind of bliss. She was mostly under and still feeling nothing when the doctors sewed her back up. She was out of it completely when she was moved to a recovery room. She was barely aware of a series of nurses looking over her, checking her vitals.

However, it was when one of the nurses stepped into the room that Mackenzie started to get a better grip on her thoughts. She reached out clumsily, trying to garb the nurse's hand, but missed.

"How long?" she asked.

The nurse smiled, showing that she had been in this situation many times before. "You've been out for about two hours. How are you feeling?"

"Like I need to hold the baby that just came out of me."

This elicited a chuckle from the nurse. "He's with your husband. I'll send them both in."

The nurse left and while she was gone, Mackenzie's eyes remained on the doorway. They stayed there until Ellington entered shortly afterward. He was pushing one of the hospital's little rolling bassinets. The smile on his face was unlike any she had ever seen from him before.

"How you feeling?" he asked as he parked the bassinet by the side of her bed.

"Like my insides have been ripped out."

"They were," Ellington said with a playful frown. "When they brought me into the operating room, your guts were in a few different pans. I know you inside and out now, Mac."

Without having to be asked, Ellington reached into the bassinet and took out their son. Slowly, he handed Kevin to her. She held him to her chest and instantly felt her heart reaching out. A surge of emotion passed through her. She wasn't sure if she had ever experienced tears of happiness in her entire life, but they came as she kissed the top of her son's head.

"I think we did good," Ellington said. "I mean, my part was easy, but you know what I mean."

"I do," she said. She looked into her son's eyes for the first time and felt what she could only describe as an emotional *click*. It was the feeling of her life being forever changed. "And yes, we did do good."

Ellington sat down on the edge of the bed. The shifting hurt her abdomen, the surgery now barely more than two hours ago. But she said nothing.

She sat there in the crook of her husband's arm with their newborn son in her arms, and could not remember a single moment in her life when she had felt such absolute happiness.

CHAPTER TWO

Mackenzie had spent the last three months of her pregnancy reading just about every book on babies she could find. There seemed to be no unequivocal answer as to what to expect the first few weeks back home with a newborn. Some said that as long as you slept when the baby slept, you should be okay. Others had said to sleep when you could with the help of a spouse or other family members who were willing to help. All of it had made Mackenzie sure that sleep would only be a precious memory of the past once they got Kevin home.

This proved correct for the first two weeks or so. After Kevin's first checkup, it was discovered that he had severe acid reflux. This meant that anytime he ate, he had to be held upright for fifteen to thirty minutes at a time. This was easy enough, but became grinding during the later night hours.

It was during this stretch of time that Mackenzie started to think about her mother. On the second night after being instructed to hold Kevin upright after feeding, Mackenzie wondered if her own mother had dealt with anything like this. Mackenzie wondered what sort of baby she had been.

She'd probably like to see her granddaughter, Mackenzie thought.

But that was a terrifying concept. The idea of calling her mother just to say hello was bad enough. But then throw in a surprise granddaughter, and that would be chaotic.

She felt Kevin squirming against her, trying to get comfortable. Mackenzie checked the bedside clock and saw that she'd had him upright for a little over twenty minutes. He seemed to have dozed off on her shoulder, so she crept over to the bassinet and placed him inside of it. He was swaddled and looked quite comfortable and she took a final look at him before returning to bed.

"Thanks," Ellington said from beside her, half asleep. "You're awesome."

"I don't feel like it. But thanks."

She settled down, getting her head comfortable on the pillow. She had her eyes closed for about five seconds before Kevin started wailing again. She shot up in bed and let out a little moan. She bit it back, though, worried that it might turn into a bout of weeping. She was tired and, worst of all, she was experiencing her first toxic thoughts about her child.

"Again?" Ellington said, snapping the word out like a curse. He got to his feet, nearly stumbling out of the bed, and marched to the bassinet.

"I'll get him," Mackenzie said.

"No…you've been up with him four times already. And I know…I woke up for each and every one of those times."

She did not know why (probably the lack of sleep, she thought idly), but this comment pissed her off. She practically lunged out of bed to beat him to the wailing baby. She rammed her shoulder into him a little harder than necessary to be considered playful. As she picked Kevin up, she said: "Oh, I'm sorry. Did he wake you?"

"Mac, you know what I mean."

"I do. But Jesus, you could be helping more."

"I have to get up early tomorrow," he said. "I can't just sit…"

"Oh God, *please* finish that sentence."

"No. I'm sorry. I just…"

"Get back in bed," Mackenzie snapped. "Kevin and I are fine."

"Mac…"

"Shut up. Get back in bed and sleep."

"I can't."

"Is the baby too noisy? Go to the couch, then!"

"Mac, you—"

"Go!"

9

She was crying now, holding Kevin to her as she settled back into bed. He was still wailing, slightly in pain from the reflux. She knew she'd have to hold him upright again and it made her want to cry even harder. But she did her best to hold it back as Ellington stormed out of the room. He was muttering something under his breath and she was glad she couldn't hear it. She was looking for an excuse to explode on him, to berate him and, honestly, just to get out some of her frustration.

She sat back against the headboard holding little Kevin as still and upright as possible, wondering if her life would ever be the same.

Somehow, despite the late-night arguments and lack of sleep, it took less than a week for their new family to slip into a groove. It took some trial and error for Mackenzie and Ellington to figure it out, but after that first week of the reflux issues, it all seemed to go well. When the meds knocked the worst of the reflux out, it was easier to manage it. Kevin would cry, Ellington would get him out of the crib and change his diaper, and then Mackenzie would nurse him. He was sleeping well for a baby, about three or four hours at a stretch for the first few weeks following the reflux, and wasn't very fussy at all.

It was Kevin, though, who started to open their eyes to just how broken the families they had come from were. Ellington's mother came by two days after they got home and stayed for about two hours. Mackenzie had been polite enough, hanging around until she realized it would be an opportune time for a break. She went to the bedroom to sneak in a nap while Kevin was preoccupied with his father and grandmother, but Mackenzie was not able to sleep. She listed to the conversation between Ellington and his mother, surprised that there seemed to be some attempt at reconciliation. Mrs. Nancy Ellington left the apartment about two hours later, and even through the bedroom door, Mackenzie could feel some of the remaining tension between them.

Still, she'd left a gift for Kevin in her wake and had even asked about Ellington's father—a subject she almost always tried to avoid.

Ellington's father never even bothered to come by. Ellington made a FaceTime call to him and though they chatted for about an hour and a few tears even came to his father's eyes, there were no immediate plans for him to come see his grandson. He'd started his own life long ago, a new life without any of his original family. And that, apparently, was how he wanted it to stay. Sure, he'd made a sweeping financial gesture last year in regards to trying to pay for their wedding (a gift they eventually denied), but that had been help from a distance. He was currently living in London with Wife Number Three and was apparently swamped with work.

As for Mackenzie, while her thoughts did eventually turn to her mother and sister—her only surviving family—the idea of getting in touch with them was a horrifying one. She knew where her mother was living and, with a little help from the bureau, she supposed she could even get her number. Stephanie, her younger sister, would probably be a little harder to track down. As Stephanie was never one to stay in a place for very long, Mackenzie had no idea where her sister might be these days.

Sadly, she found that she was okay with that. Yes, she thought her mother deserved to see her first grandchild, but that would mean opening up the scars that she had closed up a little over a year ago when she had finally closed the case of her father's murder. In closing that case, she had also closed the door on that part of her past—including the terrible relationship she'd always had with her mother.

It was odd just how much she thought about her mother now that she had a child of her own. Whenever she held Kevin, she'd remind herself of how distant her mother had been even before her father's murder. She swore that Kevin would always know that his mother loved him, that she would never let anything—not Ellington, not work, not her own personal issues—come before him.

It was this very thing that was on her mind on the twelfth night after they had brought Kevin home. She had just finished nursing

Kevin for his late-night feeding—which had started to fall somewhere between one thirty and two in the morning. Ellington was coming back into the room from having placed Kevin in his crib in the next room over. It had once been an office where they had stored all of their miscellaneous bureau paperwork and personal items but had easily become a nursery.

"Why are you still awake?" he asked, grumbling into his pillow as he lay back down.

"Do you think we'll be good parents?" she asked.

He propped his head up sleepily and shrugged. "I think so. I mean, I know you will. But me...I imagine I'll push him way too hard when it comes to youth sports. Something my dad never did for me that I always feel I missed out on."

"I'm being serious."

"I figured. Why do you ask?"

"Because our own families are so messed up. How do we know how to raise a child the right way if we have such horrible experiences to draw from?"

"I figure we'll just take note of everything our parents did wrong and don't do any of it."

He reached out in the dark and placed a reassuring hand on her shoulder. She honestly wanted him to wrap her up in his arms and spoon her, but she wasn't fully healed up from the surgery just yet.

They lay there next to one another, equally exhausted and excited for their lives going forward, until sleep took them both, one right behind the other.

Mackenzie found herself walking through rows of corn again. The stalks were so high that she could not see the tops of them. The ears of corn themselves, like old yellow teeth poking through rotted gums, peeked out into the night. Each ear was easily three feet long; the corn and the stalks on which they grew were ridiculously big, making her feel like an insect.

Somewhere up ahead a baby was crying. Not just *a* baby, but *her* baby. Already, she could recognize the tones and pitches of little Kevin's wails.

Mackenzie took off through the rows of corn. She was slapped in the face, the stalks and leaves drawing blood a little too easily. By the time she reached the end of the row she was currently in, her face was covered in blood. She could taste it in her mouth and see it dripping from her chin down to her shirt.

At the end of the row, she stopped. Ahead of her was wide open land, nothing but dirt, dead grass, and the horizon. Yet, in the middle of it, a small structure—one she knew well.

It was the house she had grown up in. It was where the crying was coming from.

Mackenzie ran to the house, her legs moving as the corn was still attached to her and trying to draw her back out into the field.

She ran harder, realizing that the stitching around her abdomen had torn open. When she reached the porch to the house, blood from the wound was running down her legs, pooling on porch steps.

The front door was closed but she could still hear that wailing. Her baby, inside, screaming. She opened the door and it opened easily. Nothing squeaked or screeched, the age of the house not a factor. Before she even stepped inside, she saw Kevin.

Sitting in the middle of a barren living room—the same living room she had spent so much of her time in as a child—was a single rocking chair. Her mother sat in it, holding Kevin and rocking him softly.

Her mother, Patricia White, looked up at her, looking much younger than the last time Mackenzie had seen her. She smiled at Mackenzie, her eyes bloodshot and somehow alien.

"You did good, Mackenzie. But did you really think you could keep him from me? Why would you want to, anyway? Was I that bad? Was I?"

Mackenzie opened her mouth to say something, to demand that her mother hand over the baby. But when she opened her mouth, all that came out was corn silk and dirt, falling from her mouth to the floor.

All the while, her mother smiled and held Kevin close to her, nuzzling him to her breast.

Mackenzie sat up in bed, a scream pushing behind her lips.

"Jesus, Mac … are you okay?"

Ellington was standing at the doorway to the bedroom. He was dressed in a T-shirt and a pair of jogging shorts, an indication that he had been working out in his little space in the guest bedroom.

"Yeah," she said. "Just a bad dream. A very bad dream."

She then glanced at the clock and saw that it was almost eight in the morning. Somehow, Ellington had allowed her to sleep in; Kevin had been waking up around five or six for his first feeding.

"Has he not woken up yet?" Mackenzie asked.

"No, he did. I used one of the bags of frozen milk. I know you wanted to save them up, but I figured I'd let you sleep in."

"You're amazing," she said, sinking back into the bed.

"And don't you forget it. Now go back to sleep. I'll bring him to you when he needs to be changed again. Fair deal?"

She made an *mmm* sound as she drifted off to sleep again. For a moment, there were still ghost images of the nightmare in her head but she pushed them away with thoughts of her loving husband and a baby boy who would be happy to see her when he woke up.

After a month, Ellington went back to work. Director McGrath had promised that he would get no in-depth or intense cases while he had a baby and nursing mother at home. More than that, McGrath was also quite lenient in terms of hours. There were a few days when Ellington left at eight in the morning and returned back home as early as three that afternoon.

When Ellington started going back to work, Mackenzie truly started to feel like a mother. She missed Ellington's help very much on those first days, but there was something special about being alone with Kevin. She came to know his schedule and quirks a bit better. And although most of her days involved sitting on the couch to heal while binging shows on Netflix, she still felt the connection between them growing.

But Mackenzie had never been one to sit around aimlessly. She felt guilty for her Netflix binges after a week or so. She used that time to instead start reading true crime stories. She utilized online book resources as well as podcasts, trying to keep her mind active by figuring out the answers to these real-life cases before the narrative reached the conclusion.

She visited the doctor twice in those first six weeks to ensure that the scar from the C-section was healing properly. While the doctors beamed over how quickly she was healing, they still stressed that a return to normalcy so soon could cause setbacks. They warned against something as common as even bending over to pick something up from the floor that had any significant weight to it.

It was the first time in her life that Mackenzie had ever truly felt like an invalid. It did not sit well with her, but she had Kevin to focus on. She had to keep him happy and healthy. She had to keep him on a schedule and, as she and Ellington had planned during the pregnancy, she also had to prepare for separating from him when it came time for him to start daycare. They had found a reputable in-home daycare and already had a spot reserved. While the provider cared for children as young as two months old, Mackenzie and Ellington had decided not to put him into care until five or six months. The spot they had reserved opened just after Kevin tuned six months, giving Mackenzie plenty of time to feel comfortable with not only Kevin's own development, but to prepare herself for the separation.

So she had no problem waiting to heal so long as she had Kevin there with her. While she did not resent Ellington for returning to work, she did find herself wishing he could be there during the day from time to time. He was missing all of Kevin's smiles, all of the cute little mannerisms he was developing, the coos and the variety of baby sounds.

As Kevin started to hit milestone after milestone, the idea of daycare began to loom larger in her mind. And with it, the idea of returning to work. The thought of it excited her but when she looked into her son's eyes, she did not know if she could live a life of running into danger, a gun on her hip and uncertainty at every corner. It seemed almost irresponsible for both her *and* Ellington to work such dangerous jobs.

The prospect of returning to work—to the bureau and anything remotely dangerous—became less and less appealing as she grew closer to her son. In fact, by the time the doctor cleared her for light exercise a little shy of three months, she wasn't sure if she wanted to go back to the FBI at all.

CHAPTER THREE

Grand Teton National Park, Wyoming

Bryce sat on the edge of the rock face, his feet dangling out into the open air. The sun was setting, casting a series of golds and bright oranges that flared into red closer to the horizon. He massaged his hands and thought of his father. His climbing gear was behind him, stowed away and ready for the next adventure. He had a hike of about a mile and a half before he'd return to his car—making a total of about six miles he had covered on foot—but for now, he wasn't even thinking about his car.

He wasn't thinking of his car, his home, or his new bride. His father had died one year ago today and they had scattered his ashes here, right off the southern edge of Logan's View. His father had died seven months before Bryce had gotten married and just a week shy of what would have been his fifty-first birthday.

It was right here, on the southern face of Logan's View, that Bryce and his father had celebrated Bryce's first full scale of the view. Bryce had known that it wasn't considered that difficult of a climb, though it certainly had been for his seventeen-year-old self that, to that point in his life, had only scaled much smaller rock faces further out in Grand Teton National Park.

Honestly, Bryce didn't see what was so special about this place. He wasn't sure why his father had requested his ashes be buried at this site. It had required Bryce and his mother to park down at the general use lot a mile and a half away from where he now sat—where, a little less than a year ago, they had scattered his father's ashes. Sure, the sunset was pretty and all, but there were lots of scenic views along the park.

"Well, I came back up, Dad," Bryce said. "I've been climbing here and there, but nothing as brutal as the stuff you did."

Bryce smiled at that, thinking of the picture he had been given shortly after his father's funeral. His father had tried Everest but had busted his ankle after only a day and a half of climbing. He'd climbed glaciers in Alaska and numerous unnamed rock formations all throughout the American deserts. The man was like a legend in Bryce's mind and that's the way he intended to keep it.

He looked out at the sunset, sure that his father would have enjoyed it. Though, honestly, with all of the sunsets he'd seen from different vantage points in his climbing years, this one was likely just a generic one.

Bryce sighed, noticing that the tears weren't coming as they usually did. Life was slowly starting to feel more natural without his dad. He still mourned, sure, but he was moving on. He got to his feet and turned to pick up the backpack with his climbing gear. He stopped short, though, alarmed at the sight of someone standing directly behind him.

"Sorry to startle you," the man standing less than three feet away from him said.

How the hell did I not hear him? Bryce wondered. *He must have been moving very quietly… and on purpose. Why was he trying to sneak up on me? To rob me? To take my equipment?*

"No worries," Bryce said, choosing to ignore the man. He looked to be in his early thirties, with a thin growth of beard covering his chin and a thin beanie-style stocking cap covering his head.

"Nice sunset, huh?" the man asked.

Bryce picked up his bag, hefted it on his back, and started moving forward. "Yeah, it sure is," he answered.

He started by the man, intending to pass him by without so much as another glance. But the man reached out and blocked his path with his arm. When Bryce tried to step around him, the man grabbed him by the arm and shoved him backward.

As he stumbled back, Bryce was very aware of all of the open space that was waiting less than five feet behind him—somewhere around four hundred feet of open space, at that.

Bryce had only thrown one single punch in his life; it had been in second grade, on the playground, when some jerk kid had told him some dumb Your Mama joke. Still, Bryce found himself making a fist in that moment, fully prepared to fight if he had to.

"What the hell is your problem?" Bryce asked.

"Gravity," the man said.

He made a motion then, not a punch but more like a throwing action. Bryce threw a wrist up to block it, realizing what was in the man's hand just as he caught the golden glitter of the sunset's reflection off of its metal surface.

A hammer.

It struck his forehead hard enough to make a sound that, to Bryce, sounded like something that might come out of a cartoon. But the pain that followed was not funny or comical at all. He blinked, absolutely dazed. He took a single step back, every nerve in his body trying to remind him that there was a four-hundred-foot drop behind him.

But his nerves were slow, the blunt attack to his forehead sending a blinding pain through his skull and a numbing sensation down his back.

Bryce crumpled, falling to one knee. And that's when the man reached out with his foot and kicked Bryce directly in the center of the chest.

Bryce barely felt the impact. His head was a blazing fire. But the kick sent him flying backward, his side striking the ground hard enough to send him bouncing back even farther.

He felt gravity claim him at once but was confused as to what, exactly, had happened.

His heart raced and his pain-filled mind went into panic mode. He tried to draw a breath as his muscles took over, flailing for any sort of purchase.

But there was nothing. There was only the open air, the wind off his descent passing by his ears and, seconds later, the briefest explosion of pain when he hit the hardpan dirt below. In the single breath left within him, he saw the red tint on the side of the wall he had just climbed, his final sunset ushering him out.

CHAPTER FOUR

What had at first felt like paradise quickly started to feel like a prison of sorts. While she still loved her son more than she could even start to explain, Mackenzie was getting stir-crazy. The occasional stroll down the block just wasn't cutting it anymore. When the doctor had cleared her for light exercise and to start picking up the pace around the house, she instantly thought of jogging or even some light weights. She was out of shape—perhaps more than she had been in over five years—and the abs she had often prided herself on were buried beneath scar tissue and a layer of fat that she was unfamiliar with.

In one of her weaker moments, she started to weep uncontrollably one night when getting out of the shower. Ever the dutiful and loving husband, Ellington had come rushing into the bathroom to find her leaning against the sink.

"Mac, what is it? Are you okay?"

"No. I'm crying. I'm not okay. And I'm crying over stupid shit."

"Like what?"

"Like the body I just saw in the mirror."

"Ah, Mac … hey, you remember a few weeks ago when you told me that you'd read that you would start crying over random things? Well, I think this is one of them."

"That C-section scar will be there for the rest of my life. And the weight … it's not going to be easy to get it off."

"And why does this bother you?" he asked. He wasn't taking the tough love approach, but he also wasn't coddling her. It was a stark reminder of how well he knew her.

"It shouldn't. And honestly, I think the crying is over something else … it just took the sight of my body to bring it all out."

"There's nothing wrong with your body."

"You have to say that."

"No I don't."

"How can you even look at this and want it?" she asked.

He smiled at her. "It's quite easy. And look … I know the doctor cleared you for light exercise. So, you know … if you let me do all of the work …"

With that, he gave a flirtatious glance back through the bathroom door and into the bedroom.

"What about Kevin?"

"Taking his late-afternoon nap," he said. "He'll probably be up in a minute or two, though. Just so happens, though, that it's been a little over three months. So I don't expect anything that happens in there to take long."

"You're such a dork."

He responded with a kiss that not only cut her off but instantly erased the way she had been feeling about herself. He kissed her deeply and slowly and in it, she could feel the three months that were pent up within him. He led her gently to the bedroom and, as he had suggested, he did all of the work—carefully and with skill.

Kevin's timing was perfect. He woke up three minutes after it was over. As they walked into the nursery together, Mackenzie pinched his butt. "I think that was a little more than light exercise."

"You feel okay?"

"I feel exceptional," she said. "So exceptional that I think I might try the gym tonight. You think you can watch little man while I head out for a bit?"

"Of course. Just don't overdo it."

And that was all it took to get Mackenzie motivated. She never half-assed anything. That included working out and, apparently, being a mother. Perhaps that was why a little over three months after bringing Kevin home, she felt guilty for going out for the first time. She'd gone to the grocery store and the doctor before, sure, but this was the first time she had headed out knowing that she would be away from her baby for more than an hour or so.

She got to the gym just after eight, so most of the crowd had thinned out. It was the same gym she had frequented when she had started with the bureau, before she had relied on the bureau's own facilities. It felt good to be back here, on a treadmill like anyone else in the city, fighting with the out-of-date resistance bands and working out just to be active.

She only managed half an hour before her abdomen started to hurt. She also had a severe cramp in her right leg which she tried to work out but to no avail. She took a break, tried the treadmill again, but decided to call it a day.

Don't even try to be hard on yourself, she thought, but it was Ellington's voice in her head. *You've grown a human inside you and then had it cut out. You're not going to go back into this thing like Superwoman. Give it some time.*

She had broken a sweat, and that was good enough for her. She went back home, showered, and fed Kevin. He was so content that he fell asleep while nursing, something the doctors advised against. But she allowed it, holding him there until she, too, felt tired. When she put him down for bed, Ellington was at the kitchen table, working on some research issues with his current case.

"You good?" he asked her as she passed back through the living room.

"Yeah. I think I might have overdone it at the gym. I'm a little sore. Tired, too."

"Need me to do anything?"

"No. Maybe in the morning help me out with some light exercise again?"

"Happy to help, ma'am," he said with a smile over his laptop screen.

She was smiling, too, when she went to bed. Her life felt complete and she had a sore cramping in her legs, the feeling of her muscles starting to learn what they had once been used for. She drifted off within a minute, freshly exhausted.

She had no idea that she'd have the dream of the huge corn-field again, of her mother holding her baby.

And, likewise, she had no idea just how badly it would affect her this time.

When the nightmare stirred her awake this time, the scream *did* come out of her mouth. When she sat up in bed, she did so with so much force than she nearly fell off the mattress. Beside her, Ellington also sat up, a gasp rising in his throat.

"Mackenzie…what is it? Are you okay?"

"Just a nightmare. That's all."

"Sounds like it was terrible. Is it anything you want to talk about?"

With her heart still hammering in her chest, she lay back down. For a moment, she was sure she could taste the dirt from the night-mare in her mouth. "Not in depth. It's just…I think I need to see my mother. I need to let her know about Kevin."

"That's fair," Ellington said, clearly still baffled by the night-mare and its effect on her. "That makes sense, I guess."

"We can talk about it later," she said, already feeling the lure of sleep. The images of the nightmare were still there with her, but she knew if she didn't get back to sleep soon, it was going to be a long night indeed.

She woke up several hours later to the sound of Kevin crying. Ellington was already starting to get out of bed, but she reached out and placed her hand on his chest. "I got him," she said.

Ellington didn't put up much of a fight. They were slowly start-ing to get back on a relatively normal sleep schedule, and neither of them were keen to start testing it. Besides, he had a meeting in the morning, something about a new case where he was going to be the lead with a surveillance team. He'd told her all about it over dinner but she had been too lost in her own thoughts. Lately, her attention had been all over the place and it was hard to focus—particularly

whenever Ellington talked about work. She missed it and was envi-
ous of him but could not quite dream of leaving Kevin just yet, no
matter how good the daycare was.

Mackenzie went into the nursery and gently took him out of the
crib. Kevin had gotten to the point where he would put a stop to
his crying (mostly) the moment one of his parents came to him. He
knew he was going to get what he needed and had already learned
to trust his own little instincts. Mackenzie changed his diaper and
then set herself down in the rocking chair and nursed him.

Her mind drifted to her parents. She could obviously not
remember feeding as a baby. But the mere idea that her mother had
once breastfed her was too much to even imagine. Still, she now
knew that motherhood brought with it a whole new filter through
which to see the world. Perhaps her own mother's filter had been
skewed—and perhaps even totally destroyed when her husband
had been murdered.

Have I been too hard on her all this time? she wondered.

Mackenzie finished feeding Kevin, thinking long and hard
about her future—not just for the coming weeks, when her maternity leave would come to an end, but to the months and years ahead
and how she might best spend them.

CHAPTER FIVE

Mackenzie's clothes were finally starting to fit again, and a few repeat trips to the gym had her feeling as if regaining her physique from a year or so ago might not be as hard as she thought. She was nearly fully healed from the surgery and she was beginning to remember what her life had been like before she had loaned out her body to the growth and development of her son.

As Mackenzie's maternity leave drew closer and closer to its end, she started to understand that it was going to be harder to go back to work than she had thought. But even before that, there was the issue of her mother to contend with. It had come up here and there in conversations with Ellington ever since she had last had the nightmare but she had made sure not to commit. After all, it was not normal for her to have a strong desire to see her mother. She usually avoided any interaction with her or even conversations about her at all costs.

But now, with only eight days remaining in her maternity leave, she had to make the decision. She had been using Kevin as the primary excuse not to make the trip, but he had been in daycare for a week now and seemed to be doing quite well with the adjustment.

Besides, in her heart, she had already made her decision. She was sitting at the bar between the kitchen and the living room, already certain that she was going to go. But actually pulling the trigger on the trip was much different than accepting the idea of it.

"Can I ask you what might sound like a dumb question?" Ellington asked.

"Always."

"What's the worst that could happen? You go, it's awkward and nothing is accomplished. You come back here to your happy baby and drop-dead sexy husband and life resumes as normal."

"Maybe I'm afraid that it will go well," Mackenzie offered.

"Now *that*, I'm not too sure about."

"What if it goes well and she wants to be a part of my life? Of *our* lives."

Kevin was sitting in the bouncer seat, staring at the little aquatic creatures mobile attached to the front of it. Mackenzie looked at him with the last comment, doing everything she could not to think of that image of her mother from the nightmares, sitting in that damned rocking chair.

"You'd be okay here with Kevin, by yourself?" she asked.

"I think I can handle him. We can have some dude-time."

Mackenzie smiled. She tried to picture Ellington the way she had originally met him nearly two and a half years ago, but it was hard to do. He had matured beyond measure, but at the same time, had also managed to become more vulnerable with her. There was no way he would have showed such a nurturing or goofball side of himself when they had first met.

"Then I'm going to do it. Two days, that's it—and that's just so I won't be constantly traveling."

"Yeah. Get a motel room. A good one, with a hot tub in the room. Sleep in. After six months of learning to be a mom and constantly adjusting sleep schedules, I think you've earned it."

His encouragement was genuine and though he had not said as much, she was pretty sure she knew why. He had essentially given up on any sort of normal grandparent scene on his side of the family. Perhaps if he could mend some fences with her mother, Kevin might have some kind of normal grandparent. She wanted to ask him about this but decided not to. Maybe after she got back and knew whether the trip had been a bust or not.

She grabbed her laptop, sat on the couch, and went online to purchase her tickets. When she finished filling everything out and hit that final mouse-click, she felt as if the weight of the world had been lifted from her shoulders. She shut the top of the laptop and let out a sigh. She looked down to Kevin, still in his bouncer seat, and gave him a bright smile, sticking her nose out at him. She was rewarded by a slowly dawning smile.

"Okay," she said, looking back at Ellington. He was still in the kitchen, cleaning up from dinner. "Tickets purchased. My flight leaves tomorrow at eleven thirty in the morning. You okay to pick little man up from daycare?"

"Yes. And that will start two days of absolute man-fueled debauchery. I'm afraid neither of us may ever be the same."

She knew he was doing his best to keep her thinking positive. It was helping to some extent, but her mind was already on something else—one last errand she wanted to tackle before leaving DC.

"You know," she said, "if it's okay with you, I might get you to drop him off at daycare, too. I think I need to speak with McGrath."

"You finally make a decision about that, too?"

"I don't know. I want to go back. I don't know what the hell else I would do with my life, honestly. But... being a mother... I want to give Kevin what I never had when it came to a parent, you know? And both of us working as FBI agents... what kind of a life would that be for him?"

"This is all heavy stuff," he said. "I know we've talked it out a few times before, but I don't think it's a decision you need to make right now. I think you're right; talk it over with McGrath. You never know what that man is thinking. Maybe there are ways around it. Maybe a... I don't know... maybe a different role?"

"As in, no longer an agent?"

Ellington shrugged and came over to sit beside her. "That's why I feel like I can actually understand what you're going through," he said, taking her hand. "I literally can't see you being anything other than an agent."

She smiled at him, hoping he knew just how good he was at knowing exactly what to say. It was just the boost she needed to pick up the phone and place a call to McGrath after hours. She hadn't done it much in her career—and never when it wasn't about a case—but she felt the urgency of it all of a sudden.

And it only grew stronger as she listened to the phone start to ring in her ear.

She fully expected McGrath to be irritated by meeting with her at such an early hour. But when she found his office door already open at eight o'clock, McGrath was already perched behind his desk. He had a cup of coffee in his hands as he went over a small stack of daily reports. When he looked up to her as she entered, the smile on his face looked genuine.

"Agent White, it's so good to see you," he said.

"Likewise," she said, taking a seat on the opposite side of his desk.

"You look well rested. Is the baby finally on a normal sleep schedule?"

"Normal enough," she said. She already felt awkward. McGrath was not one who typically engaged in small talk. The idea that he truly was glad to see her back in the building crossed her mind and made her feel almost guilty for the reason behind the meeting.

"Okay, so you asked for this meeting, and you have about half an hour before my next one," he said. "What's going on?"

"Well, my maternity leave is up next Monday. And if I'm being honest, I don't know if I'm ready to come back."

"Is it a physical thing?" he asked. "I know healing from a C-section can be exhausting and take a great deal of time."

No, that's not it. The doctors have basically cleared me for just about everything. If I'm being honest, I just feel torn about what to do." She was alarmed to feel the stinging of tears at the corners of her eyes.

Apparently, McGrath saw them too, and felt for her. He did his best to appear casual as he leaned forward and spoke, looking away to give her the dignity of wiping her tears away before they escaped.

"Agent White, I've been with the bureau for almost thirty years now. In my time here, I've seen countless female agents get married and have children. Some of them left the bureau or, at the very least, took on a role with less risk. I can't sit here and tell you that I understand what you're going through because that would be a lie. But I *have* seen it. Sometimes it was with agents I would have never expected to walk away. Is this sort of where you're headed?"

She nodded. "I want to come back. I miss it…more than I care to admit, really. I honestly don't even know what I'm asking for. Maybe a few more weeks? I know that's sort of asking for special privilege or whatever, but I just can't make this decision right now."

"The best I can do is to give you another week. If you want it. Or you can come back and I can just assign you something of a desk job. Research, numbers, mobile surveillance, something like that. Would that interest you?"

Honestly, none of it interested her. But at least it was something. It was McGrath giving her the proof she needed that there were options available to her.

"Maybe it would," she said.

"Well, take the weekend to think it over. Maybe get away somewhere and sort out your thoughts."

"Oh, I'm going somewhere, all right. Back to Nebraska for a visit."

She wasn't sure why she had told him that. She wondered if McGrath had always been this easy to speak to or if he perhaps had some kind of softer aura about him, making him more approachable. It was weird. She'd only been away for three months and McGrath suddenly seemed like a different person—more caring, more friendly.

"Good to hear it. Leaving Ellington alone with the baby? Isn't that a bit brave?"

"I don't know," she said with a smile. "He seems to be looking forward to it."

McGrath nodded politely but it was clear that his mind was elsewhere. "White…did you ask for this meeting to ask my advice? Or just to get a gauge on how I might react if you told me you were thinking of walking away?"

She only shrugged as she answered: "Maybe a bit of both."

"Well, I can say without a doubt that I'd much prefer for you to stay. Your record speaks for itself and, as much as I hate to admit it, your instincts are almost supernatural. I've never seen anything quite like it in all my years with the bureau. I do believe it would be an absolute waste for you to leave your career behind at such an early age. On the other hand, I've raised two children—one boy and one girl. They're both grown now, but raising them was one of the most enjoyable and rewarding experiences of my life."

"I had no idea you had kids," she said.

"I tend not to talk too much about my personal life while at work. But in a case like this, with something as valuable as your career on the line, I don't mind giving you a behind the scenes peek."

"I appreciate that."

"So ... go enjoy your weekend back home. Do you want to meet again on Monday to figure out what comes next?"

"That sounds fine," she said. But Monday seemed every far away. Because as she got up from the chair, she knew that her next stop was the airport. And after that, she'd be back in Nebraska.

As she made her way back through the FBI building, she felt as if she were setting a trap for herself. For most people, the ghosts of their pasts tended to haunt them. But as she prepared to head back to Nebraska to meet with her mother, Mackenzie felt as if she was not only awakening those ghosts, but giving them ample opportunity to prepare for their haunting.

CHAPTER SIX

It was one fifteen Nebraska time when her plane landed in Lincoln. She had spent the bulk of the flight trying to plan out how the trip would go. But it wasn't until she heard the wheels squealing on the landing strip that she knew she simply needed to pull the bandage off and get it over with. She could still enjoy that night to herself in a luxurious motel room—which she had already booked. And she could do it after getting the hard part out of the way.

She'd used bureau resources in a kind of sketchy way to find out that her mother was still working in the same position she had been when they'd crossed paths a little over a year ago. She was still part of the cleaning crew at a Holiday Inn located in the small town of Boone's Mill. And as it just so happened, Boone's Mill was two hours away from Belton, the little town she had grown up in—a town she planned to visit before she headed back home.

Another urge struck her as she sidled up to the rent-a-car station in the airport twenty minutes later. She knew that about half an hour from this very airport was the building where she had started her career as a detective. She thought of the man she had worked with for nearly three years before the FBI had courted her—a man named Walter Porter who, somewhere behind his distaste of having to work with a woman and his ingrained sexism, had actually taught her a great deal about what it took to be an effective enforcer of the law. She wondered what he was up to. He'd likely be retied by now, but being back here, so close to the station, made her want to catch up with him.

One scab at a time, she told herself as she collected the keys from a grouchy woman behind the counter.

Once she got on the road, Mackenzie pulled up the number to her mother's Holiday Inn, just to make sure she was working. As it turned out, her shift ended in half an hour, which would put Mackenzie about an hour outside of being able to meet her mother at the hotel. That wasn't too big of a concern, though, as Mackenzie also had her mother's home address to go by.

She was surprised to find that the flat land and familiar atmosphere of Nebraska calmed her significantly. There was no anxiety or fear about meeting her mother. If anything, the open land and sky made her miss Kevin. When she realized that she had not been away from him for this long, her heart sagged in her chest. For a moment, it was hard to breathe. But then she thought of Ellington and Kevin, together in the apartment as the day came to a close. Ellington was an outstanding father, in ways that were still surprising her on a daily basis. She started to understand that perhaps Ellington needed this time alone with his son just as badly as she needed this time to venture back into her past to try to mend bridges with her mother.

If these are the emotions all parents go through, she thought, *maybe I have been giving my mother too hard of a time.*

Of all of the thoughts that had been rolling through her head as soon as she had stepped foot on the plane in DC, it was this one that brought tears to her eyes. She knew her father had dealt with a few of his own demons, though the nature of them had been vague at best because her mother had never trashed him in front of her or Stephanie. Mackenzie tried to then apply that to the fact that her mother had been left a widow, with two girls to raise. It was very possible (and this was something Mackenzie had considered before) that she'd held such a high opinion of her father because he had died when she'd been young. As a young girl, she'd had no reason to doubt him or to see him as anything other than her own personal hero. But what about the mother who had tried to raise two girls, ultimately fail, and then receive the scorn of not only most of the community, but one of her own daughters as well?

Mackenzie managed a thin smile through the tears as she wiped them away. She wondered if these thoughts were suddenly becoming so clear because now she, too, was a mother. She'd heard about women changing many facets of their attitudes once they had a child but had never really considered it. But here she was, living proof of that theory, as she felt her heart begin to soften for a woman she had essentially demonized for most of her life.

Nebraska rolled by outside of the car, ushering Mackenzie back to her past. And for the first time since leaving the state, she found herself nearly eager to step back into that past and let the cards fall where they may.

Patricia White lived in a two-bedroom apartment six miles away from the Holiday Inn where she worked. It was located in a small complex that was not quite run down but definitely in need of some maintenance and attention. Mackenzie held her phone in her hand, the address and apartment number on her screen courtesy of some underhanded bureau resource use.

When she approached her mother's second-floor apartment, she did not hesitate at the door or freeze in her thoughts as she had expected. She knocked right away, doing her best not to think about it too much. The only real question was how to start the conversation... how to ease into the waters rather than jumping in and dog-paddling uselessly.

She heard footsteps approaching after a few moments. When the door opened and she saw the look of surprise on her mother's face, *that's* when Mackenzie froze up. She wasn't sure when she had last seen her mother smile, so the one that spread across her face made Mackenzie feel like she was looking at a different woman.

"Mackenzie," her mother said, her voice thin and excited. "Oh my God, what are you doing here?"

"I had some time off and figured I'd come out and say hello." It wasn't a total lie, so she was okay with it for the time being.

"No call first?"

Mackenzie shrugged. "I thought about it, but I also knew how it would go. Besides … I just needed to get away for a while."

"You okay?" She sounded genuinely concerned.

"I'm fine, Mom."

"Well, come in, come in. The place is a wreck, but hopefully you can look past it."

Makenzie stepped inside and saw that the place was not a wreck at all. In fact, it was quite tidy. Her mother had decorated minimally, making it easy for Mackenzie to spot the old picture of her and Stephanie sitting on the small end table by the couch.

"How have you been, Mom?"

"Good. Very good, actually. I've been saving up some money here and there, so I was finally able to get out of debt. I got a promotion at work … it's still not much for a job, but the money is better and I manage a few ladies on the crew. How about you?"

Mackenzie sat down on the couch, hoping her mother would do the same. She was thankful when she did. She had never been a believer in saying *You might want to sit down for this* because it was far too dramatic.

"Well, I do have a bit of news," she said. She started the slow process of opening up Photos on her phone and scrolling for a particular picture. "You know that Ellington and I got married, right?"

"Yes, I know. Funny that you still call him by his last name. Is that like a work thing?"

Mackenzie couldn't help but chuckle. "Yeah, I think it is. Are you mad you missed out on a wedding?"

"God no. I hate weddings. That might be the smartest decision you've ever made."

"Thanks," she said. Her nerves were bubbling like lava as the next words came out of her mouth. "Look, I came out here because I have something else to share with you."

With that, she held out her phone. Her mother took it and looked at the picture of Kevin in his little hospital blanket, two days old just before they left the hospital.

"Is this …?" Patricia asked.

"You're a grandmother, Mom."

The tears were instantaneous. Patricia dropped the phone to the couch and put her hands over her mouth. "Mackenzie … he's precious."

"He is."

"How old is he? You look too good to have just had him."

"A little over three months," Mackenzie said. She looked away from the slight sting of pain that crossed her mother's face. "I know. I'm sorry. I wanted to call sooner, to let you know. But after that last time we talked … Mom, I didn't even know if you'd want to know."

"I get that," she said right away. "And it means the world to me that you showed up to tell me in person."

"You're not upset?"

"God, no. Mackenzie … you could have never told me. I would have never known the difference. I think I was fully prepared to never even see you again and … and I …"

"It's okay, Mom."

She wanted to reach out to her, to take her hand or embrace her. But she knew anything of the sort would feel forced and strange to both of them.

"I got a new blender last week," her mother said, out of nowhere.

"Um … okay."

"You drink margaritas?"

Mackenzie smiled and nodded. "God, yes. I haven't had a drink in about a year."

"Are you nursing? Can you drink?"

I am, but we've got enough stored up in the freezer."

Her mother made a confused face but then burst into laughter. "I'm sorry. But this is all so surreal … you having a baby, storing breast milk …"

"It *is* surreal," Mackenzie agreed. "And so is being here. So … where are we on those margaritas?"

✤ ✤ ✤

"It was your last visit up here that did it," Patricia said.

They were sitting on the couch, each holding a margarita. They sat on opposite ends, clearly still not comfortable enough with the situation.

"What about that visit?" Mackenzie asked.

"You weren't overly rude or anything, but I saw how well you were doing. And I thought to myself, *she came from me*. I know I wasn't a great mother…not at all. But I *am* proud of you, even if I didn't have much to do with the way you turned out. It made me feel like I could make something of myself, too."

"And you can."

"I'm trying," she said. "Fifty-two years old and finally out of debt. Of course, working at a hotel isn't the grandest of careers…"

"Are you happy, though?" Mackenzie asked.

"I am. More so now that you've come to visit. And told me this wonderful news."

"Ever since I closed Dad's case…I don't know. If I'm being honest, I think I just tried to push any thought of you right out of my head. I figured if I could put what happened to Dad in the past, I might as well put you there, too. And I was fully prepared to do that. But then Kevin came along and Ellington and I realized that we weren't really giving our baby much of a family beyond the two of us. We want Kevin to have grandparents, you know?"

"He has an aunt, too, you know," Patricia said.

"I know. Where *is* Stephanie?"

"She finally went ahead and made the move to LA. I don't even know what she's doing, and I'm afraid to ask. I haven't spoken to her in about two months."

Hearing this stung Mackenzie a bit. She had always known that Stephanie was something of a loose cannon when it came to any kind of stability in life. But still, she rarely stopped to think that Stephanie was yet another daughter who had chosen to live a life mostly detached from her mother. Sitting there on the couch, margarita in hand, it was the first time Mackenzie had ever bothered to wonder what it must be like for a mother to know that both of her children had decided that their lives would be better off without her in them.

"I feel like I should tell you I'm sorry," Mackenzie said. "I know I pushed you away pretty much after Dad's funeral. I was only ten, so maybe I wasn't aware that's what I was doing, but…yeah. I just kept doing it for the rest of my life. And here's the thing, Mom…I want Kevin to have a grandmother. I really do. And I hope you might want to work on getting there with me."

Patricia was again choked up by tears. She leaned crossed the couch, closing the distance between them, and wrapped her arms around Mackenzie. "I wasn't there, either," Patricia said. "I could have called or made some kind of an effort. But when I realized you had checked out—even as a kid—I let it go. I was almost relieved. And I hope you can forgive me for that."

"I can. Can you forgive me for pushing you away?"

"I already have," Patricia said, breaking the hug and sipping from her margarita to stem the flow of tears.

Mackenzie could feel her own tears coming on, and she wasn't quite ready to be *that* open in front of her mother. She stood up, cleared her throat, and downed the rest of her drink.

"Let's get out of here," she said. "Let's grab dinner somewhere. My treat."

A look of disbelief crossed Patricia White's face which was slowly dissolved by a smile. Mackenzie could not remember ever seeing her mother smile so wide; it was like seeing a different person. And maybe she *was* a different person. If she gave her mother a chance, maybe she would find that the woman she had pushed away for so long was not quite the monster she had convinced herself she was.

After all, Mackenzie was definitely a different person than she had been at ten. Hell, she was a different person than she had been a little over a year ago when she had last spoken with her mother. If having a baby had taught Mackenzie anything, it was that life could change pretty quickly.

And if life itself could change so quickly, why not people?

CHAPTER SEVEN

Mackenzie woke up the next morning with a very gentle hangover. Reconnecting with her mother over dinner had been nice, as had the few drinks they'd had afterward. Mackenzie had made it to her hotel room—the luxurious one she and Ellington had agreed upon—and slipped into the hot tub with a bottle of wine she had ordered from room service. She knew the two extra glasses she'd had while relaxing in the tub might be a bit too much, but she figured she deserved it after gestating a human being in her womb and having to forgo alcohol the entire time—not to mention the additional time without a drink while she was actively breast-feeding and pumping.

The slight headache she had as she got out of bed and started to get dressed was a small price to pay. It had been nice to be alone after slowly starting to mend things with her mother. They had caught up, shared some stories, shared some pains, and then called it a night. With plans to reconnect in a week or so, after Mackenzie had gotten back home and decided what to do about work, there was only one other thing on Mackenzie's list of things to do while visiting Nebraska.

She felt like she had come full circle. Traveling here alone, seeing her mother, relishing the wide open spaces the state had to offer. Even though she was not one for sentiment, she could not ignore the draw to go back by her old station—the station where she started her career as a detective almost six years ago.

After grabbing breakfast, she did just that. It was an hour and a half drive from her hotel in Lincoln. Her plane did not leave for

DC for another seven hours, so she had plenty of time. She honestly didn't even know why she was going. She had not cared much for her supervisor and, as ashamed as she was to admit it to herself, she could barely remember anyone she worked with. She did, of course, remember Officer Walter Porter. He had served as her partner for a small stretch of time and had been by her side during the Scarecrow Killer case—the case that had eventually attracted the attention of the FBI and their pursuit of her.

All of the memories came trickling back as she parked her car across the street from the station. It looked so much smaller now, but in a way that made her proud to know it. More than nostalgia, it was a heartwarming familiarity.

She crossed the street and stepped inside, unable to stop the smile from touching the corner of her lips. The small entryway led to a receptionist-type desk, which was paneled in with a sliding glass. Behind the woman sitting at the desk, a small bullpen of sorts was set up and looked exactly the same as it had when Mackenzie had last stepped foot in the building. She approached the glass, delighted to find a familiar face, albeit one she had not thought of in a very long time, sitting behind the glass.

Nancy Yule looked as if she had not aged a bit. She still had the pictures of her kids perched at her desk, and the same little plaque by her phone, reciting a bit of scripture that Mackenzie could not remember.

Nancy looked up and it took her a few seconds to realize who had just walked in the door. "Oh my God," Nancy said, getting to her feet and rushing to the door on the far side of the paneled wall. The door came open and Nancy came rushing out, capturing Mackenzie in a hug.

"Nancy, how are you?" Mackenzie said in the grip of the hug.

"Same old, same old," Nancy said. "How are *you*? You look fantastic!"

"Thanks. I'm good. I just came out to visit my mother and thought I'd stop by to see my old haunts before I headed back home."

"Is home still in DC?"

"It is."

"Still with the bureau?"

"I am. Sort of living the dream, I don't mind saying. Got married, had a child."

"I'm so happy for you," Nancy said, and Mackenzie didn't doubt she meant it. A little flicker of sadness came to her face, though, when she added: "Though, I'm not so sure your visit here is going to be prove very happy. Just about everything around here has changed."

"Like what?"

"Well, Chief Nelson retired last year. Sergeant Berryhill stepped up and filled in his place. Do you remember him?"

Mackenzie shook her head. "No, I can't say that I do. Hey, would you happen to have an address or phone number for Walter Porter? I have a number for him but it hasn't worked in quite some time."

"Oh, sweetie, I forgot you were his partner there for a while. I…. well, I hate to be the one to tell you this, but Walter died about eight months ago. He had a pretty massive heart attack."

"Oh," was all that Mackenzie could think to say. She also wondered if she was a terrible person for not being too terribly saddened by the news. Honestly, though, he seemed like nothing more than a passing acquaintance at best.

"That's terrible," she said. She glanced back through the glass, into the bullpen and the hallways beyond where she had spent nearly five years of her life. This was the epicenter of where she had made her first arrest, solved her first case, pissed off her first male supervisor numerous times.

They were all fond memories, but they felt like nothing more than faded photographs.

"There might be a few officers out on patrol that you once worked with," Nancy commented. "Sauer, Baker, Hudson …"

"I don't want to interrupt anyone's day," Mackenzie said. "I was really just taking a walk down memory lane and—"

The buzzing of her cell phone from her pocket interrupted her. She grabbed for it instantly, assuming it would be Ellington with a story about something cute Kevin had done—or some medical issue. Their baby boy had been healthy for his entire three and a half months of life and they were just waiting for that first doctor's visit.

But the name she saw on her display was absolutely not one she had been expecting while on her little sabbatical out to Nebraska. The display read **McGrath**.

"Excuse me, Nancy. I need to take this."

Nancy gave a little nod and stepped back through the doorway toward her desk as Mackenzie took the call.

"This is Agent White."

"Based on how you're answering the phone, can I assume you're going to stay with us?" McGrath said. There was no humor in his voice. If anything, it almost sounded as if he were trying to convince her.

"Sorry. Habit. I still don't know yet."

"Well, maybe I can help. Listen…I respect what you're going through and appreciate the honesty you showed in my office the other day. But I'm calling to ask you something of a favor. Not a favor, really, because it's technically part of a job you still have. But I got a call about a case an hour or so ago. It's in Wyoming, so it's out your way. And since you just happen to be out there, I thought I'd give you first crack at it. Seems like an easy one. You may not have to do much more than show up, check out a crime scene, and question a few people."

"I thought you said you respected the conversation we had in your office."

"I do. Which is why I'm offering you the case first. You're already out that way, it looks to be simple…and I figure it could be a good test to see if your heart is still in it. You've also recently worked another case that was sort of similar from the looks of it. If you say no, that's perfectly fine. I can get someone out there as soon as tomorrow morning."

The feeling of her life coming full circle washed over her again. Here she was, standing in the station she had started out in as a hopeful officer with ambitions of being a detective—ambitions that she achieved in a very short time. And now here she was, speaking to a director with the FBI not even seven years later.

She looked to the other side of the glass, to the desks and offices and hallways. It was easy to see that space and recall the sense of purpose she'd had back then. She still felt it, but it was quite different as a cop just starting out, a woman on a force that was primarily men, wanting to make a difference in the world.

"How simple are we talking?" she asked.

"There's suspicions that someone is pushing people to their deaths off of popular climbing sites. The latest one was in Grand Teton National Park. So far, there are believed to be two victims."

"How do we know these aren't just typical rock-climbing accidents?"

"There's evidence of violence before the falls."

Already, Mackenzie's thoughts were sorting themselves out, trying to come up with answers even at this early stage. And because of that, she knew what her answer for McGrath would be. It had been nearly eight whole months since she had last done anything considered *active* in regards to her job; the amount of excitement that quickly overtook her as she gave her answer was welcome, but unexpected.

"Send me the case details and trip itinerary. But I want to be back home within two or three days."

"Of course. I don't see that being a problem. Thanks, Agent White. I'll send everything I have to your e-mail."

Mackenzie ended the call and felt as if she were standing in the middle of a very surreal dream for a moment. Here she was, standing in the first police station she'd ever worked in, ruminating on her past and trying to sort out her future. And now there was this call from McGrath, this unexpected case coming out of nowhere in the middle of it all. It felt like the universe was trying to sway her in her decision-making.

"Mackenzie?"

She was torn away from the absurdity of it all by Nancy Yule's voice. She smiled and shook her head. "Sorry. Zoned out for a bit."

"Seemed like an intense call," Nancy said. "Is everything okay?"

Mackenzie surprised herself a bit when she nodded and said: "Yes. I think everything is just fine, actually."

CHAPTER EIGHT

Seven hours later, she was in the sky somewhere over northern Nebraska, headed for Wyoming. Everything had happened so quickly that she had not had a chance (or any proper location available) to print out the materials that McGrath sent over to her concerning the case out at Grand Teton National Park. Because of that, she was forced to go over all of it on her iPhone.

There honestly wasn't too much to go over. The police reports were scant at best, as were the forensics reports. When a body fell from such a height, the cause of death wasn't typically debated all that much. She scanned the documents several times but found nothing—not because of her own skills, but because of a lack of information. Even the details she'd received on the victims wasn't much to go on. Two people had been involved in fatal rock climbing accidents, but there was evidence to suggest that they may not have been accidents at all. There was a severed rope involved in one of the cases, and a wound on one of the bodies that did not seem to line up with injuries expected from a fall.

Mackenzie made some notes in her phone, wondering if the father had some sort of tie to the cause of his son's murder. It wasn't much to go on but given the lack of information she had, at least it was something.

As the plane made its descent into Jackson Hole airport, Mackenzie was able to look out her window and see the peaks of mountains from Grand Teton National Park. It was quite beautiful in the crisp blue sky of the evening, making the idea that there might be a killer running rampant down there all the more unnerving.

The sight also stirred an ache in her heart—an ache for Kevin. She felt like a failure for leaving him behind, like a heartless mother who had already placed certain priorities over her child. But she had read more than enough information on this sort of thing; she knew that such feelings were typical for new parents. Still, it didn't make the feeling any less real.

When she stepped off of the plane several moments later, she didn't quite feel like she was on a case. She had come into Jackson Hole in the same clothes she had been wearing when she had walked into the police station and spoke to Nancy Yule. She had obviously not packed her bureau attire for her trip to see her mother, nor had she packed her service weapon. This was something she'd have to sort out with the local PD. Hopefully there would be no hold-ups because there was no FBI field office in Wyoming; the office out of Denver covered the states of Colorado and Wyoming.

This realization made her feel like she was in the middle of nowhere—a feeling that only intensified when she stepped into the airport. It was a nice enough airport for sure, but the thin stream of bodies moving through it made the bustle of Dulles back in DC absolutely chaotic.

It was the lack of human traffic walking through the concourse that made it very easy for Mackenzie to see the woman standing at the end of her gate, dressed in police blues. She looked to be about forty or so, her blonde hair hitched up in a ponytail to reveal a pretty and angular face. She seemed to be watching each and every person that got off of Mackenzie's flight. When they locked eyes, the female officer nodded politely and met Mackenzie on the concourse floor.

"Are you Agent White?" the woman asked. The silver tag above her left breast identified her as Timbrook.

"I am."

"Good. I'm Sergeant Shelly Timbrook. I figured I'd meet you here and save you the trouble of renting a car. Besides … the sooner I can get you out to the site, the better. The second victim—a twenty-two-year-old male named Bryce Evans—was found at the bottom of

Logan's View and since that's located within the park, there's the worry of the public eye and all that."

"How far from here is the park entrance?" Mackenzie asked.

"Not even ten minutes. Add another five to that to get us to Logan's View."

"Then lead the way," Mackenzie said.

Timbrook took the lead and headed for the airport exit. Mackenzie followed behind, texting Ellington to let him know that she had arrived and met with local PD. When she had called to tell him about the call from McGrath, he had already known; he said McGrath had called him right after he'd gotten off the phone with her. Ellington had seemed excited for the opportunity, claiming it seemed just like the sort of thing she'd need to get focus.

The hell of it was that he was right. And she wished he could be there with her. Not only was it the longest she had been away from Kevin since he'd been born, but she and Ellington had not spent any more than ten hours apart ever since her maternity leave had started one month before Kevin had arrived.

She missed him. It made her feel far too young and immature, but it was the truth. But she managed to push it to the side for now. She'd make sure to Facetime him and Kevin whenever she was able to check into a hotel. But based on the terrible lack of information in the police reports, she suspected she was in for a rather long afternoon.

"I'll go ahead and get this out of the way," Timbrook said. "I'm sort of a fan of yours. I know that sounds stupid. But when that whole Scarecrow Killer thing went down in Nebraska a couple year years ago, that was impressive. Do you mind me asking … is that how you ended up with the FBI?"

"More or less."

"It was refreshing to see you—a young woman—take charge of a force that was primarily men. Made me feel good."

Mackenzie wasn't sure how to handle that sort of compliment, so she skipped it entirely and went straight to business.

"I've studied the reports on both of the victims and there's very little there," she said. "I know the second victim was only discovered yesterday, but why the hold-up on any details for the first victim?"

"Because for the first half a day or so, everyone assumed it was just a tragic accident. Or maybe a suicide. I was even thinking along those lines myself. The body was found at the bottom of Exum Ridge. Mostly likely had been there for several days."

"How far apart at Logan's View and Exum Ridge?"

"It's about two and a half miles. There are a few central trails that run between the two."

"And the murders are believed to be about four days apart, right?"

"As far as we can tell. That's based on that the coroners are saying. You have to keep in mind…both bodies were discovered by hikers. We have no way of knowing for sure how long the bodies had been there. Speaking to family and putting together the schedules of the victims, we can only come up with a pretty good idea, but nothing absolute."

"Can you walk me through what you know of the first victim?"

"Sure. A woman named Mandy Yorke, twenty-three years of age. Her body was discovered at the base of Exum Ridge. She was a good distance away from any of the normal advertised climbing spots, indicating that she was something of a pro. It happens a lot…climbers that get quite good don't stick to the traditional climbs. They'll go off the beaten path to find something more challenging. That's why it was assumed her death was an accident. But when we started looking over the evidence from the crime scene, we saw that her climbing rope had been cut."

"Intentionally?"

"Sure looked like it. It was a clean cut. We compared it to some old broken ropes at the park. The difference in appearance. A rope that had been frayed and Yorke's clean-cut one were very different."

"Any idea *where* the rope was cut?"

"At the top. It's as if the killer was waiting there, waiting for Yorke to reach the top and then cut it."

"Any sabotaged equipment from the second victim?" Mackenzie asked.

"None that we could find. The coroner says we got lucky—*we* as in the investigators—because the victim fell on his back. It allowed us to clearly see the blunt trauma to the head that we are quite sure was not caused by the fall. It looked like he'd been attacked or possible bludgeoned. A rock or a hammer, maybe."

"Is the entire force on board with this theory?"

"Hardly," Timbrook said. "The coroner has yet to verify that the injury to the second victim's brow was *not* cause by the fall. But just looking at it... well, it tells the story. But that's not quite good enough, as you know. And while most everyone agrees that the cut to Yorke's rope does indeed look very clean, not many are ready to consider foul play either. Climbing accidents aren't uncommon. We get about three or four deaths a year as a result of hiker and climber accidents, and somewhere around fifty injuries."

"But two deaths in four or five days?" Mackenzie asked.

"I know. I think just about everyone on the force is suspicious but no one wants to go there just yet... not until it's an absolute certainty."

Mackenzie nodded slowly. She understood the hesitancy to call two deaths *murders* when there was no hard evidence. But perhaps more than that, she understood where Timbrook was coming from as well. Mackenzie had been there—the soft-spoken female officer in a sea of men who, while they might respect her, were usually slow to take her ideas as truth. While she certainly realized that equality was becoming more and more the norm in law enforcement, she also knew that some traditions were hard to break out of.

As Timbrook drove into the entrance of Grand Teton National Park, Mackenzie got a better feel for the size of the place. She assumed the peaks she had seen from the airplane had been part of the park. She also started to understand that in a place of this scope and size, security was likely a mere handful.

Timbrook took them down a side road that appeared to be used primarily for park vehicles. She then turned off about a mile further down and pointed the car down a smaller road, one that was just barely wide enough for two lanes of traffic—one coming, one going. There were rails to either side, protecting cars from some pretty serious drops over the edge.

"I think victim number two was killed *after* his climb. We went up to the top of Logan's View and saw some odd marks right along the edge of the summit."

"How high up is it?" Mackenzie asked.

"Four hundred and twenty feet. Which is why we're driving straight to the top. Besides, I feel like that's where the killer struck."

Mackenzie watched the small mountain rises sweeping by, scatterings of trees here and there only partially blocking views. After about five minutes on the road, Timbrook skillfully taking a series of sharp turns, the land started to flatten out. The road gave way to a strip of hard-packed dirt that came to an end in a makeshift parking lot. There was a large square of gravel and dirt, bordered with concrete stops one each end indicating parking spots. Timbrook pulled in behind one of these concrete blocks and parked the car. They both stepped out into the gravel, Mackenzie once again taking in the view. It seemed that none of the immediate mountain ranges were very high. She supposed this made this area quite popular for climbers—both professional and aspiring.

And we know plenty about that, don't we?

The thought came out of nowhere, like some rip current from the back of her mind. It made her pause for a moment, her head going swimmy as memories of the past tried to overcrowd her mind. A spike of fear stabbed at her heart for a moment and then it was gone.

"Agent White? You okay?"

"Yes, I'm fine. I assume we have a hike ahead of us?"

"Yes, but nothing huge. The hiking entrance to Logan's View is only about half a mile that way," she said, nodding toward the left. There was a very thin trail snaking its way between a few trees, leading into the scant growth. Most of the tree line was thin, making the views a little more spectacular.

They did very little talking as they covered the space between the parking lot and the end of the trail. It was an easy hike, but one that Mackenzie enjoyed. It sure beat the DC streets and the treadmill at the gym. She supposed this was the first force exercise she'd endured since giving birth to Kevin ... and it felt exquisite.

The trail came to an end almost abruptly, spitting them out at what Mackenzie thought was a gorgeous view. More of the park was visible, unobstructed and stretched out far and wide. The point known as Logan's View sat about fifty yards away from the tree line. The panoramic view was only blocked off by a single thin rail that looked as if it had been placed there only to fulfill some safety obligation and nothing more. Almost right away, at the edge of the tree line, there was a posted sign stating that all adults needed to keep their children close and that anyone below the age of ten was strongly suggested to stay behind the protective rail.

A stream of yellow crime scene tape had been tied to the sign's post, streaming all the way across to the nearest tree, blocking most of the access to Logan's View.

Mackenzie followed Timbrook under the tape and to the rail. When she saw Timbrook step easily over it, Mackenzie felt something in her stomach shift. Nervousness? Fear? She wasn't sure. All she knew was that it took an extra bit of mental prodding to force herself to follow Timbrook over that damned rail.

Once she was on the other side, there was perhaps ten feet of perfectly flat ground. While Mackenzie did not enjoy the thought of peering down at the drop, she could not deny the stunning view. She looked away from the wide-open vista, to the ground directly in front of her. She noticed that Timbrook had stepped aside, letting her get a better look at the scene.

The ground was covered in a very thin layer of grass, but it was the hardpan that was dominant. She assumed that being this close to the edge of the mountain, it would be harder for grass roots to thrive and grow. Because of this, it was quite easy to see recent signs of some sort of conflict. There were scuffed footprints and, about two feet away from the edge, two droplets of something dark enough to probably be dried blood.

"Was there any climbing gear found at the site?" Mackenzie asked.

"No. We spoke to his family and his wife. They were both able to describe the sort of climbing gear he owned. But we never found it. Not up here and not down there. We assume the killer stole it."

"Was it expensive gear?" Mackenzie asked. "Any chance he was killed *for* the gear?"

'Highly unlikely. I think it was just basic gear. Standard stuff you could get at any sporting goods store. And not much of it. The climb up here to Logan's View isn't a very hard one from what I understand. Not that I could do it..."

Yeah, that makes two of us, Mackenzie thought. Faintly, she thought of a case about fifteen months ago. She remembered climbing up a water tower in pursuit of a killer and feeling some very old feelings coming back to her heart and mind—fears and worries from her past that she thought she had buried under so much mental rubble that they would never see the light of day again.

But here, at the top of the four-hundred-twenty-foot-high Logan's View, she felt those fears rumbling. In her mind's eye, she imagined a horror movie where a zombie's hand was breaking through the topsoil under which it had been buried.

"I assume there aren't any security cameras up here?" she asked.

"None. Once you get beyond the primary entrance, the information center and gift shop, there are no cameras."

Mackenzie checked each of the clear scuff marks on the dirt. They were too old—as well dusted over and vague—to make out any sort of clear identifying marks. She looked at the two small dark drops two feet away from the edge and was confident that it was indeed dried blood.

That close to the edge, she could not help herself. She looked over. She moved slowly, craning her neck so the rest of her body could stay as far away from the edge as possible.

The drop took her breath away. For a moment, she felt dizzy. She wanted to pull herself back away from the view quickly but also did not want to alarm Timbrook. There was one frightening moment as she came back away from the edge, her heart in her throat, where Mackenzie thought she might vomit.

"How accessible is the area where the body was found?"

"Easier than this," Timbrook said, looking out at the view in much the same way Mackenzie had.

"How soon can I get photos of the scene before the body was removed?"

"As soon as we get you to the station."

As they headed back to the car, Mackenzie decided that she liked Timbrook quite a lot. She was driven and straight to the point. It was clear that she felt more strongly about a possible murder scenario than most of the others on her force. And the quicker she could get stable ground for such an approach, the smoother the case would be.

And Mackenzie wanted a smooth case. The faster she closed this, the sooner she would make it back to Kevin and Ellington. Thinking of them sent a little pang of sorrow through her heart as she got into the car and Timbrook carried her back down the side of the mountain.

CHAPTER NINE

The bottom of the mountain had revealed exactly what Mackenzie had been expecting: a whole lot of nothing. She and Timbrook spent less than five minutes looking over the area where Bryce Evans had fallen to his death. Without a body there to help spell out the story, the scene itself was essentially useless.

Still, it was unnerving to know that someone had fallen from such a height. Mackenzie looked up, craning her neck and imagining the fall. It sent little twirls of anxiousness through her stomach—not too dissimilar form the feeling of Kevin kicking her in the stomach before he'd been born.

"You seem discouraged," Timbrook said on the way back to the station.

"No, not really," Mackenzie said. "It's always a little hard to play catch-up when all I have to work with is cleaned crime scenes and photos and files."

"Well, it wasn't much help when the body *was* there. Everyone was so set on it being an accident. There may as well have not been a body there at all."

Mackenzie wanted to comment on how she was accustomed to that. There were plenty of memories fresh in her mind about being undermined by those she worked for—especially following her trip back to Nebraska. But she said nothing, not wanting to add that level of toxicity to the situation.

When they arrived at the station, an officer met Timbrook at the door. He was an average middle-aged African-American man who looked to be about forty or so. He gave Mackenzie a little nod and smile as he updated Timbrook on several other local tidbits that did not include the two rock-climbing deaths. He was about to step away when Timbrook grabbed his arm and kept him still.

"Officer Waverly, I want you to meet Agent White," Timbrook said. "Agent White, Waverly has been running most of the legwork on the rock-climbing cases. He's also very well versed in the ins-and-outs of the park. He's about the only other person in the place that thinks they are both hands-down murder cases."

Waverly extended his hand, and Mackenzie shook it. "Have you formed an opinion yet?" he asked.

"I'm getting there," she said. "Why don't the two of you give me everything you know about the case?"

Timbrook was quite eager to do this very thing, quickly leading her to a room near the back of the station. There were two tables, one on either side of the room, already littered with a few files and folders.

Timbrook and Waverly were quiet as Mackenzie looked over the case files, speaking only when she asked them a question. Mackenzie spent a little extra time and attention on the photos from Bryce Evans's fall site. Timbrook kept busy by looking at a map of the Grand Teton National Park pinned to the wall, while Waverly scrolled through a series of e-mails on his phone.

The photos were difficult to look at. They weren't grisliest Mackenzie had ever seen, but they were right up there. As Timbrook had said, Evans had landed on his back. That had obviously caused some serious damage to his limbs and the back of his head. From the look of the corpse, his back and ribs had basically been pulverized upon impact. The blood flow from the back of the head was minor, but she suspected that was because most of it had run either beneath or directly around the body.

But it was the man's forehead that she paid the most attention to. Just above the left eyebrow, there was a visible wound. She supposed he could have struck his head somewhere during the fall on the way down, but the wound looked too crisp for that. One of the photos showed the wound close up. It looked slightly like an indentation, the bottom of it rounded and the top not quite as clear. Whatever it was, it was impossible to miss; there was a divot in the man's head that looked to be at least an inch or two deep.

"Any idea how deep this wound is?" Mackenzie asked.

"It's in the coroner's report," Waverly said. "Nine centimeters at its deepest. There was a clear sign that his skull had been dented and fractured."

"We keep coming back to that," Timbrook said. "Any idea what it might be?"

"I don't know. Maybe some sort of climbing equipment. I could possible the rounded end of some sort of carabiner hook or something." But even as she said this, that didn't seem to fit. She figured you'd have to get a hell of a lot of force behind your attachment to do that sort of damage with a carabiner.

Mackenzie finally slid the gruesome photos away and started looking over the police files. There wasn't much more information than what she had already read on the flight into Jackson Hole, though a few hand-jotted notes gave her some more insight.

"Other than immediate family, who has been questioned?" she asked.

"We've questioned Bryce Evans's wife and Mandy Yorke's roommate," Timbrook said. "From what we can see, there's no connection between them. The only similarity we can find between them is a love of rock climbing."

"You said Evans was married. What about Yorke? Any significant other in the picture?"

"Not according to the roommate," Waverly said. "She said Mandy was sort of an introvert. Said she wasn't the type to really date."

Among the files, there was also an evidence bag. In it, Mackenzie found a newer model iPhone. She slid it out and looked to Timbrook and Waverly for authorization.

"You're good," Timbrook said. "It's been looked over and permanently unlocked. Help yourself."

Mackenzie did just that. She scrolled through about a month's worth of e-mails and call history. The only thing of interest she found in the e-mails was a confirmation e-mail to a 5K race Mandy had signed up for. She then went into photos and found over seven hundred of them. Most of them were of scenic hiking trails, interspersed with some climbing shots and selfies. She could feel the eyes of Timbrook and Waverly on her as she looked, perhaps hoping she'd find something that they had overlooked.

After about five minutes, she *did* notice something. And it came from one of the last pictures that had been taken. She tapped back a few times, coming to the Photos screen that told when a picture was taken. The picture that had caught Mackenzie's eye had been taken four days ago—the same day Mandy had died.

"Do either of you know if she went climbing solo that day?" she asked. "Did she have a partner?"

"Pretty sure it was a solo climb," Timbrook said. "Her roommate said that it was very rare that Mandy climbed with anyone. Said she felt it slowed her down." Timbrook's face slowly washed over with interest as she leaned forward and asked: "Why?"

Mackenzie showed them the second to last picture that had been taken with Mandy Yorke's phone. It was a selfie—or so it seemed it first. In the picture, Mandy Yorke was smiling brightly at the camera, her face perfectly centered with only a bit of the background showing. The background was the granite surface of some great wall behind her. But the angle was all wrong and the camera looked like it was a little too far away from her face to be a selfie.

Unless Mandy Yorke was double jointed and had freakishly long arms, there was no way she had taken the picture herself.

"Someone was with her," Mackenzie said. "When she went out to climb four days ago, she had a partner."

Both Timbrook and Waverly looked at the picture again. Waverly went so far as to tilt his head to the left, trying to see it from a different angle.

"Damn," Timbrook said.

She took the phone and scrolled back a few pictures. It had been taken on the same day, during the morning if the soft light of the sun was any indicator. In the picture, a young man of about twenty to twenty-five years of age was posing, giving an exaggerated thumbs-up sign. He was dressed down, in a tank top and a pair of athletic shorts.

"Maybe him?" Timbrook said.

"Only one way to find out," Mackenzie replied.

Before Mackenzie even began to give instruction, Timbrook and Waverly got to their feet, already headed for the door to get an ID on the man in the picture.

It took less than five minutes to get an ID on the man in the picture. One phone call to Mandy Yorke's roommate was all it took, but Waverly followed up by texting the photo in question to the roommate to get final confirmation. Mackenzie had an address ten minutes after finding the picture and wasted no time heading out to locate the man from the picture—twenty-one-year-old Malcolm Morgan.

Morgan lived in Jackson Hole, just a fifteen-minute drive from the police station. Mackenzie invited Waverly to ride along. She felt there was no real danger in the visit, but was very aware that she had not been actively on a case in nearly eight months. And while Timbrook had secured a gun for her—a standard police-issued Glock—Mackenzie also had to admit that she was not exactly comfortable with the thought of handling it.

To Mackenzie, it still didn't quite feel like she was legitimately on a case. She was dressed casually and it was hard to find the urgency of it all. It wasn't getting back into the mindset of an agent that was difficult; it was finding the groove of realizing that yes, she was indeed back to work now and the life she had known before Kevin was again front and center.

When she and Waverly arrived at Morgan's apartment, Waverly parked, finishing up a conversation with Timbrook, who was back at the station compiling a list of local climbing instructors and enthusiasts. Malcolm Morgan lived in a quaint part of town, just far enough from the more scenic areas to seem almost typical. He lived in a second-floor apartment with one of the many mountain views scattered along several points within the city.

As it just so happened, Mackenzie spotted Morgan as she got out of the car. He was entering the building with two bags of groceries, absorbed in the task of not dropping the one in his right hand.

"I think you can stay out here," Mackenzie told Waverly. "If two of us approach him, he's going to get spooked. I'll let you know right away if things go bad."

"You sure?"

Mackenzie nodded and closed the door. She crossed the parking lot and entered the apartment building about twenty seconds after Morgan had stepped inside. She skipped the elevator in the lobby, opting for the stairs. When she came to the second floor and started down the hallway, she spotted him again. Morgan was apparently getting home for the day, unlocking his apartment door while juggling his two bags of groceries as Mackenzie approached him.

Morgan nearly dropped one of the bags as he fumbled with his keys. Mackenzie hurried forward, not only trying to be nice, but to take him off his guard. It might be a sneaky trick, but it would be a good way to see how quickly his demeanor changed when she told him why she was there.

"Let me help you," she said, taking the nearly fallen bag.

Morgan, startled, looked up at her. His surprise was quickly replaced with gratitude as he smiled at her. "Thanks. I appreciate that."

He got the door unlocked and then opened it. Mackenzie handed the bag over to him as he gave her a scrutinizing look.

"You live here?" he asked.

"No. I'm actually here to see you."

"Me?"

"Yes." There was a moment where she panicked a bit, worried that she had left her badge and ID in her bag. She'd nearly not even carried it with her when she had packed for Nebraska, but she had eventually included it—out of habit more than anything else. She then felt the familiar shape of it in her back pants pocket. She took it out, showing it to Morgan. "I'm Agent Mackenzie White, with the FBI. I was hoping to ask you some questions about a young lady named Mandy Yorke."

The response was immediate. Morgan's face went slack and for a moment, he looked as if someone had literally punched him in the stomach.

"Well, that saves me the trouble of asking if you knew her," she said.

"I, um…well, I haven't really spoken to anyone about her since she died," he said. "And…why is the FBI on this? Didn't she just fall?"

"We don't know. There are lots of questions we have. That's why I'm here. See…as far as we knew, Mandy was by herself when she had her accident. But the photo history on her phone suggests that not only did you see her that day, but that you were likely with her during that last climb."

The look of shock had never left his face, but it thickened as she said this. Morgan had not invited her in, but the few sentences they had spoken to one another had led them both through the door. For the time being, Morgan seemed fine with that.

"Photos?" he asked.

"Yes. There's one of you dressed like you might be headed out for a climb or a run or something. And then, a few hours later, there's a photo on her phone. It appears to be a selfie at first, but then it becomes apparent that someone else is holding the camera. So my questions to you is: What did the two of you do on the day she died? And if you indeed partnered with her on her climb, why did you not come forward?"

Morgan let out a sigh and dropped his grocery bags to the floor. When something broke inside one of them—a glass jar of some kind, by the sound of it—he seemed to not care. He then leaned against his kitchen counter as if wrestling with something.

"Malcolm, do you know what happened?"

What she was really looking for was any sort of guilt response. If it turned out that this guy was responsible for cutting Mandy's line, she'd be back home much sooner than she had thought.

"Yeah, I climbed with her. For a while. I didn't go all the way up. That's why I never stepped forward when I heard she'd had an accident. I know how *convenient* that sounds on my part. But I swear... I only went halfway up with her. I think she planned to climb the rest of the way."

"And this was on Exum Ridge?"

"No. Well, not my part of the climb. We um... well, we've sort of been seeing each other. And we had this spot we liked to stop at. It's sort of this weird little cove-like area tucked into a crevice in the side of a wall some of the local climbers know as Exum Gate. That's as far as I went with her that day."

"Mandy's roommate said Mandy wasn't seeing anyone."

"Well, yeah, I don't guess she would have told her roommate. We were keeping it quiet. I—damn, this is bad. Look... I have a girlfriend. A fiancée, actually. She's going to UCLA. I've been seeing Mandy on the side for a few months now. It wasn't really anything serious... but serious enough for me not to want my fiancée to find out."

There's the guilt, Mackenzie thought, though it was not the sort of guilt she had been hoping for.

"Had you climbed with her before?"

"Yeah, eight or nine times. We found our little spot on Exum Gate on the fourth one."

"And why did you stop there on the day she died?"

"The same reason we stopped the other times," he said, starting to blush a bit. "It's long enough to lay down, secure enough so you know you won't fall. We'd sleep together up there. That day would have been the fourth time. I know it sounds perverted, but sex at that height... knowing those big open spaces are just a few feet behind you..."

Not wanting to hear any of the specifics, Mackenzie pressed on. "So why did you not go the rest of the way with her that day?"

"We sort of had a fight. Not a fight...just an argument. She said she didn't want to do it anymore...me and her, messing around. She didn't want to be second choice. I understood it but...well, I wasn't ready to give her up. So I argued with her a bit, saying maybe I could call off the engagement. She said that only proved what type of man I am. And then she asked me to leave her alone. After that, I rappelled back down and she stayed there, in our little spot. I looked up a few times on my way down, but never saw her come out."

"This place on Exum Gate...how hard is it to get over to the Exum Ridge climb?"

"Not hard at all if you know what you're doing. You just have to climb up a bit more and then scale over to the left a few hundred feet. There's a little ledge there along the face that's wide enough to make an easy transition most of the way. Not really ideal for novice climbers, but easy enough if you've got some experience."

"When did you hear she had died?"

"I still haven't officially been told. Keep in mind, we weren't telling anyone. Not even her roommate knew. I saw it on Facebook."

"How did the two of you meet?"

"At a climbers' meet-up a few months ago. Nothing official, just this get-together by a small climbers' group on Facebook."

"How often do these meet-ups take place?"

"About once every few months for this one group. But there are several of them around here. I don't know how many of them meet, though."

Mackenzie made a mental note of this, wondering if these groups might be worth exploring a little deeper.

"Why did you not come forward when you heard she had died? You were very likely the last person who ever saw Mandy alive."

"I thought about it, actually. But what the hell was I going to say? If I had gone to the authorities, all it would accomplish is having to come clean about my affair while also making it public knowledge that Mandy was screwing around with an engaged guy right before she died. That doesn't look good for either of us. Besides...like I said. We were just fooling around; it wasn't anything serious."

"Where did you go when your rappelled back down?"

"Back home. Here. I had a lot of work to get done."

"Did you stop anywhere between Exum Gate and here?"

Morgan took a moment to think about it and Mackenzie did not think he was simply stalling. He was starting to show some genuine concern at this point, doing what he could to not only help but also ensure that he stayed out of trouble.

"Yes," he finally answered. "I stopped by Starbucks. That was all, though. I came back here and worked the rest of the day."

"And what do you do?"

"I do advertising for small businesses."

"So you would have an e-mail trail of your work for that day?"

"Yes. Although I don't know when I would have sent the first one. If you're looking for some sort of alibi, I mean."

"We'll cross that bridge when we get there. Please just stay in town for the next few days. We may need to question you again or potentially look at your phone and computer."

"Of course. Whatever I can do."

Mackenzie thanked him for his time and then made her exit, fairly certain that Malcolm Morgan was not the killer. And even though he hadn't had any solid information, his story did give a better picture of what Mandy Yorke's life had been like leading up to her death.

She thought back to standing on the edge of Logan's View and looking down earlier. It had brought something to mind, something she had pushed down and tried her very best to forget. But she felt it trying to rise to the surface, trying to take center stage to remind her that—new mother and rising FBI agent or not—she still had some demons to face. And it looked like she'd have to face them by herself, more than half a country away from her family and any sort of support system.

CHAPTER TEN

When she returned to the station with Waverly, she found Sergeant Timbrook in the conference room again. She was sitting hunched over in a chair, changing into a different set of shoes. Having not been expecting such a sight, it was slightly funny to Mackenzie.

"Is this a bad time?" Mackenzie asked.

"Not at all," Timbrook said with a chuckle. "Some of us are headed out to Exum Ridge in a few minutes. A park guide called in and said they'd discovered a little side winding trail that looked recently disturbed. I was going to call you before we headed out. I'm changing shoes because there's a bit of a hike involved."

"That's perfect," Mackenzie said. "That was going to be my next stop. Mind if I catch a ride?"

"Not a problem at all," Timbrook said, lacing up her pair of sneakers.

Mackenzie was wearing sneakers as well, yet another reminder of how unorthodox this situation was. It was hard to stay in the agent mindset without the usual attire. Yes, she had her badge and ID, but without the clothes and her sidearm, it felt quite weird indeed.

The ride out to Exum Ridge was a short one, Timbrook driving them back into the park and then sketching along the boundaries of it. They parked in a lot that was similar to the one situated behind Logan's View. This time, the hike ahead of them looked to include a drastic slope that was heavily populated with trees. Mackenzie looked at it with skepticism, wondering if she was physically fit enough to do it. She *felt* like she was in shape but she had to remind herself that the C-section had heavily affected her core strength.

There were five of them in all as they started climbing the trail that would lead them to Exum Ridge. Timbrook led the way, followed by Mackenzie and Officer Waverly. Behind them were two other policemen—a younger officer named Petry and a tall gaunt man Timbrook had introduced as Deputy Miller. Miller kept mostly quiet but his posture and staunch face made it clear that he did not appreciate having to make such a climb. Mackenzie wondered if he was among the many in Timbrook's office who believed both recent deaths had been nothing more than accidents.

Mackenzie did her best to focus on staying alert and aware of her own limitations. She assumed McGrath had figured there was no way she'd be doing anything as grueling as this when she came out to check on this case. It was frustrating because the hike would not have affected her at all a year or so ago. But she could feel the weakness in her abs and the hesitancy in her once-strong legs. She knew they were still strong, but they had been out of commission for a while—and a few trips to the gym over the last few weeks simply wasn't cutting it.

"The fact that people do this for fun," Waverly said, "blows my mind."

Behind him, Deputy Miller grunted. Mackenzie looked over at him and noticed that he was sweating. She then looked back to the ground, ignoring the protests of her legs and the uneasiness in her abdomen.

It took them fifteen minutes to get to a stretch of land that was mostly flat. It led to yet another incline, this one not as steep and much easier to traverse.

"Over here," Waverly said. "I think this is the trail they were suspicious of."

Everyone walked over to look at where he was pointing. Mackenzie saw a very thin trail that led down into the forest, starting with a downhill pitch that leveled out about twenty feet down and wound ahead of them toward Exum Ridge.

"You mind checking it?" Mackenzie asked Waverly. "Look for any signs of someone rushing through—maybe even of an altercation. I imagine this is going to dump out pretty close to Exum Ridge, so we should be seeing you soon."

Waverly looked to Timbrook for guidance, and she nodded. Waverly gave a little nod and started down the trail, taking the downward slope carefully.

"How much further to Exum Ridge?" Mackenzie asked.

"Maybe another five minutes," Timbrook said.

Mackenzie did her best to hide her discomfort as they soldiered on further down the hiking trail. On occasion, she'd catch sight of Waverly further off to the right, partially hidden by trees and deadfall as he made his way down the sketchier trail. Using him to distract her from the pain in her legs and abdomen, she was relieved when they came to the end of the trail much sooner than she expected.

They all stopped and looked up at Exum Ridge. It loomed upward like some giant sentinel. Although Mackenzie knew that it was just a little over seventeen hundred feet high, she could easily envision it puncturing a hole in the sky from where she stood.

"So this is Exum Ridge," Timbrook said. "Exum Gate is about two hundred feet over that way," she said pointing to the right.

"But this is where Mandy Yorke's body was found?"

"That's right," Miller said, stepping up closer to the first drastic incline that quickly became a mountain in front of them. "Right here. She landed face down, with her right leg caught under her, cleanly broken in half. I've seen a few accidents out here on these peaks, but this one was the worst."

"Any idea how experienced Yorke was?"

"Well, I'm not exactly a rock climber, so I wouldn't know a novice from an expert," Timbrook said. "That's why Petry came along today. He's the go-to on that sort of thing."

"You climb?" Mackenzie asked.

"Yeah, but just for fun," Petry said. "I'm not obsessed like some of the people that come out here. That climb over from Exum Gate to right here would be a little too scary for me."

Mackenzie looked up to the rock face in front of her and looked to the right. Exum Gate was about two hundred feet over, angled upward. Looking up in that direction made Mackenzie's head feel a little swimmy. She felt those memories from the past come rushing forward, now blaring like the horn of some big truck that was about to run her over.

Behind that horn, there were other murky things … coming in waves, crashing on the shore and then being pulled back out.

"… you have to get it done. Just be careful and you can do it. It's easy. You can …"

Swirling earth below her and the only thing she could see clearly was the blood.

And she had to get down, had to get down quickly and …

Mackenzie shook the memories away, feeling confident that they were so close that she could rope them down at any time if she chose to do so. For now, though, there was the rock wall right in front of her, the junction between Exum Gate and Exum Ridge.

"Officer Petry, the police report said that there were several pieces of gear recovered at this very spot. Do you recall what they were?"

"A length of rope, several carabiners, and her helmet. It was all easy to identify because there were initials in magic marker on the underside of the helmet: M.Y."

"Mandy Yorke," Timbrook said.

Mackenzie again looked up to the rock wall in front of them. She wasn't quite sure what she was looking for. If Mandy Yorke had fallen to her death, there would be nothing this low to tell what had happened. Still, as she scanned upward, she saw several small outcroppings along the edge of the wall. A few of them would make getting started quite easy—after, of course, making it the first twenty feet or so without any assistance.

She thought she saw something on one of those outcroppings—a small ledge that jutted out from the wall about two feet from the looks of it.

"Timbrook, I need to double-check my eyes," she said. She pointed up at the little outcropping, squinting her eyes. "You see something right there?"

Timbrook followed Mackenzie's finger and nodded slowly. "Yeah. There's something up there. Looks...orange, maybe? It's too hard to see from here."

Mackenzie looked around to see if anyone had brought any climbing gear, already knowing the answer. She then looked back up at the outcropping and her heart started to thrum in her chest. Slowly, she took a step forward toward the wall.

What the hell are you doing?

It was a fair question. She *knew* what she was doing and with each step, those memories grew stronger and stronger.

The world, swirling below, her feet dangling. The shape of her instructor on the ground down below, doing his best to remain strong so she wouldn't freak out.

"You can do it, Mackenzie. Don't let the fear get to you. You know what to do. You can get down. You can—"

"Agent White?"

She looked back to a concerned Timbrook. She then shrugged and crouched down, rubbing her hands in the dirt along the ground. When she had a nice grimy coating of dirt and dust, Mackenzie approached the rock wall and glanced up to the object on that little outcropping.

Now that she was standing directly beneath it, she estimated it to be about twenty or twenty-five feet overhead. The rock wall that led to it was not smooth at all, providing plenty of textured areas, crags, and crannies for convenient footholds. She reached up for the first one, her hand trembling slightly and her heart basically in her throat.

"Agent White," Timbrook said again. "What the hell are you doing?"

Mackenzie thought about chasing a murderer around the perch of a tall water tower somewhere in her recent past. But her mind delved even further back than that, seeing her own dangling feet and an injured instructor beneath her, bleeding on the ground.

"It's okay," Mackenzie said, looking back at the lower rock wall of Exum Ridge. "I used to do this. And I was pretty damned good at it."

With that, Mackenzie sank her fingers against the first available handhold and started to climb.

Right away, she found that it was easier than she expected. The first few handholds and footholds were well worn, likely the result of countless kids trying to see how far up they could get before their parents scolded them. But after about ten feet or so, it became trickier. Mackenzie had to search for grips and scramble with the soles of her well-worn Nikes—not the best footwear for scaling the side of a mountain.

When she was about two arm lengths away from the outcropping with the orange object, she thought of Ellington. These memories that were resurfacing were new to her in a way, bringing back a chunk of her early life that she had blotted out somehow. Because of that, it was not a part of her past she had ever shared with Ellington.

Oh my God, he'd freak out if he saw me right now.

She smiled, but it was fleeting. Because on the heels of that thought were those old memories, snapping at her heels like a rabid dog.

Rope burns on her palms, ambulance sirens, her mother showing up drunk out of her mind, a policeman telling her that she had probably saved her instructor's life...

"Nope," she said out loud to herself. "Not right now. No thank you."

She fought the urge to look down and instead craned her neck up, looking for another handhold. There was a convenient one just a bit out of her reach but she was able to reach it with a good, long stretch. Her abdomen ached and she grimaced as she pulled herself up.

The outcropping was not large enough to rest on, but she was able to support herself by her right arm, taking some of the pressure off of her legs and abdomen. As she braced herself against the littler ledge, she could clearly see the orange shape that she and Timbrook had spotted down below. She grabbed it with her free hand and looked it over.

It was standard belay device, often used by people climbing without a partner. It wasn't a very sophisticated piece of equipment but it still took some fairly basic climbing knowledge to operate it, maintaining the rope as a climber made their way along the rock.

She looked down for the first time to the four officers below; apparently, Waverly had come back out of the forest from the thin trail and joined them in the time it had taken her to reach the device.

"It's a belay device," she called down. She turned it over in her hand and saw the same initials Petry said they had found on the underside of the Yorke's helmet: M.Y. "It's Mandy Yorke's," she added.

Making sure everyone had eyes on her, she tossed the device down softly. She then wasted no time getting back down the wall. She was sweating a bit but she felt confident the grime she had placed on her hands would keep her safe. She found that getting back down was easier than going up. She remembered the trickier areas along the wall and took them easily. It again brought to mind that picture from her past but she tucked it away before it could properly frighten her.

She felt instantly relieved when she was back on the ground. Still, she looked back up the short little route she had just taken and could not deny that she had enjoyed it.

"Petry, do you recall anything in particular about the ropes that were found?"

"Just that there was a fray in it, pretty clean."

"Any sort of knots stand out to you?"

Petry shook his head, clearly not happy that he had no real answer to give. "None that I can recall."

"If that's Yorke's belay device," Miller said, "what does it tell us?"

"It tells us that a woman that was apparently a rather good climber dropped her belay device—a rather important piece of equipment when climbing alone. It could happen, for sure, but not often." She considered something for a moment and then added: "I'd like to get a look at the rope. Is that possible?"

"Absolutely," Timbrook said. "You think we might have missed something?"

"It's too early to know for sure," she said.

But then she looked back up at that little outcropping she had just been resting on—and at the thousands of feet above it. Mackenzie *did* have a theory, but she wanted to see the ropes first. She was working her way through the theory as they walked back down to the parking lot. The hike down the stretch was much easier on her than the one going up.

And while she was able to proceed without too much of the discomfort she had experienced on the way up, the growing memories started to wear on her now. They were front and center in her mind, demanding that she face them, demanding to know why she had blocked them out of her mind.

"You probably saved his life, young lady," the paramedic had told her as he wrapped up the rope burns on her palms. "Your instructor might very well owe you his life…"

CHAPTER ELEVEN

Mackenzie, Timbrook, Waverly, and Petry all stood around a table just outside of the evidence room at the back of the Jackson Hole police station. Everything they had found from the area where Mandy Yorke's body had been found was spread out on the table. The orange belay device had been included, recently tagged and catalogued by Petry.

Looking at the ropes Mandy had been using when she died, Mackenzie felt her theory snap into place and prove itself correct. She picked up the rope and fed it through her hands until she came to a knot she had seen a few times but had never employed herself.

"This knot...it's referred to as a Munter hitch. It's sort of a fail-safe rope—complicated to make but simple to use. But climbers typically only use it when there's no other options. It's primarily only used in emergencies."

"Such as someone dropping their belay device?" Timbrook asked.

"Yeah."

"So what exactly does that mean?" Waverly asked.

"Well, I still find it interesting that a trained climber with skills like Mandy Yorke was clumsy enough to drop her belay device. This Munter hitch knot sort of backs it up, though. It's usually only used in extreme cases. And if you put those two things together, it tells me that Mandy Yorke was trying to come down Exum Ridge in a hurry."

She then found the area in the rope that had been severed. As she had been told, it was a clean cut. It was not frayed or somehow torn jaggedly by relentless use. It had been cut cleanly.

"So you firmly believe we can rule out simple accidents as the cause of death?"

"For Mandy Yorke, without a doubt."

Petry took a step away from the table, looking back and forth between the pieces of evidence. He looked uneasy, like he was looking for any excuse to leave the room.

"What is it, Petry?" Timbrook asked.

"This is going to cause a shit storm."

"I'm used to navigating shit storms," Mackenzie said. "Let me guess. There's pressure on the local PD to keep any rumors of a killer away from the public due to concerns of lower park attendance and revenue. Something like that?"

"*Exactly* that," Timbrook said. "It's one of the reasons I'm getting so much grief from the sheriff and his little peons about trying to label it as a murder case. It's also one of the reasons, I think, he's choosing not to waste his time with the case. The less he knows, the less involved he can be."

"And if it turns out to be a string of murders," Waverly said, "he can blame the lack of information to the public on the sergeant he put in charge."

Timbrook nodded sadly and the look in her eyes made Mackenzie once again think of the time she had spent in Nebraska as a detective. She really wanted to think times had changed since then—that Timbrook was *not* getting the run-around because she was a small-statured and attractive woman. But really, at the root of it, Mackenzie was pretty sure that's exactly what was going on.

"You think it was the same killer at both sites?" Timbrook asked.

"Wait, hold on," Petry said. "That seems like one hell of a stretch."

Mackenzie bit her tongue, but she was pretty sure those above Timbrook had something of a mole assisting her with the case. Sure, Petry was apparently the go-to on rock climbing information, but it was clear that he was doing everything he could to keep denying that they could very well be looking at two murders committed by one person.

"Can you tell me how it's a stretch?" Mackenzie asked.

"Look...let's give you the benefit of the doubt and say that there *was* some sort of foul play involved with Mandy Yorke. That does not mean we can cast that same scrutinizing eye at the death of Bryce Evans."

"I saw scuff marks in the dirt at the top of Logan's View as well as a dent in the victim's head that suggest otherwise."

"He fell almost thirteen hundred feet," Petry exclaimed. "Of course he's going to have some dents in his head."

Mackenzie sighed and then looked Petry in the eye. He looked away almost at once—an action that told her he would back down pretty easily if things were to escalate into an actual argument.

"I appreciate the train of thought you're implying," she said. "And it's clear that you want this solved just as badly as everyone else. But I was called in to assist on this case, meaning it is now under FBI jurisdiction. As seeing as how I'm the only federal agent on the case, it's basically my show. Trust me...I hate pulling the FBI card, but I will if I have to."

She paused here, letting this sink in, making sure he wasn't going to try to talk her down. When he remained quiet, Mackenzie went on.

"Based on what I'm seeing with Yorke's rope and Evans's forehead, as well as the site of where I believe he was pushed, we will not be pursuing this as two murder cases. While I'm not fully prepared to say it was the work of the same person, I am heavily leaning that way. I'm happy to discuss my thoughts and theories, but I will not tolerate relentless questions. Is everyone okay with that?"

Timbrook and Waverly nodded in unison, Waverly going so far as to say: "One hundred percent."

But Petry only looked at each one of them for a few moments and then gave a defeated nod of his head. "Yeah," was all he said as he walked quickly for the door and took his leave.

"Sorry about Petry," Timbrook said. "He's actually a great police officer, but he's also one of the boys. Worse than that, he sort of looks up to the older generation, the old farts that still look down on little old me, wearing a badge and being in charge of a few things around here."

"Every station has a few of them, I suppose," Mackenzie said. "Now…you two know the area much better than I do. Do we have names and addresses for the next of kin for either of the victims?"

"Well, like you saw in the reports, Mandy Yorke has no family in the area. Her parents were both killed in a car accident when she was seventeen. The grandmother that raised her after that is in a retirement home in California. The orderlies say that when they informed her that Mandy had died, she was unresponsive. They say the poor woman can barely remember her own name most days."

"And what about Bryce Evans?"

"His mother lives just outside of town. His father passed away about a year ago. When I spoke with his mother just after his death, she told me that Bryce had probably gone up there for sentimental reasons. She said it was where they spread his ashes."

"Did she seem open to helping?" Mackenzie asked. "I'd like to speak with her myself."

"Yeah, I can make that call," Timbrook said. She then left the room, presumably to do exactly that.

Mackenzie looked back at the items on the table: the helmet, the back cracked and basically obliterated; the rope, severed near one end and with a Munter hitch knot several yards away from the cut.

In her mind's eye, Mackenzie envisioned Mandy Yorke rappelling down the side of Exum Ridge, looking up and seeing someone up at the top. Maybe with a knife, maybe staring down at her with a maniacal smile. And all there was beneath her was wide open space.

"You can do it, Mackenzie," she heard in her head.

And upon hearing it again, she remembered what it was like to be hovering there in open space, nothing but open air beneath her feet and the knowledge that one wrong move could potentially end her life.

It was all the motivation she needed. Sore abs and legs be damned, she was going to find out who had killed Mandy York and Bryce Evans.

Janelle Evans looked rather well put-together to have just lost her son. That was Mackenzie's first reaction, anyway. But within a few minutes, she realized that it was all a front. The woman was in pain. She was trying to mask her grief with makeup and a plastic smile. But there was nothing in her eyes—no sparkle, no glint, nothing. The wine glass sitting on the coffee table just before noon suggested that Mrs. Evans was masking her grief in several different ways.

She'd answered the door as if it were any other day, greeting Sergeant Timbrook warmly. When Mackenzie introduced herself, Mrs. Evans looked slightly shocked but shrugged it off as she led them into her living room.

Mackenzie looked around for any sign of recent grieving: photo albums, spent tissues, anything. But Mrs. Evans apparently kept a very tidy home and was trying to hide any signs of her sorrow. Mackenzie didn't quite understand it, but she did know that people chose to deal with their grief in various ways. Who was she to judge how this woman chose to respond to the tragic death of her son?

"Mrs. Evans, I'd like to ask you a few questions about Bryce. Would that be okay?"

"I've already told Sergeant Timbrook and her folks everything I know, but I suppose so. Have there been new developments?"

"Well, Mrs. Evans," Timbrook said, "when we last spoke, there was another case that we were looking into. I did not mention it at the time because there was no direct link—and there may still not be one. But it's similar enough for us to take precautions. There was another climbing-related death three days before Bryce's accident. We need to start looking at both cases from a different angle."

"Are you... are you thinking someone did this on purpose?" It was the first time Mackenzie had seen Mrs. Evans visibly rattled since she had opened the door for them.

"We aren't one hundred percent certain," Mackenzie said, "but it is a strong enough suspicion that we have to look into it. Which is why I'd like to ask you some questions."

"Of course," she said. There was now something in her eyes— some faraway look that made it appear that she might fall asleep at any moment.

"For starters, you told Sergeant Timbrook that Bryce had climbed up to Logan's View as a sort of remembrance. For his father, is that correct?"

"Yes. He mentioned it to me the day before he went. I guess I decided not to really listen. It always terrified me to know that he was rock climbing. Such a foolish and dangerous thing to do in my opinion."

"Do you know how long he had been rock climbing?"

"Well, it was about five or six years ago when his father took him climbing to the top of Logan's View. A bonding thing. I guess it was probably two years or so before that when he started to practice, you know? Something to do with his dad on the weekends. Bryce never really did much climbing after his father died, though. He was still active...just not as enthusiastic. He mainly did smaller climbs, just stuff to stay in shape. He was very private about it."

"Do you know if he ever climbed with a partner?"

"No one consistent. He had a friend that did it for a while, but he moved. I think he went to some meet-up thing last year—a meeting with other climbers. There was one other guy he climbed with for a while but that petered out."

"Do you know anything in particular about this meet-up?" Mackenzie asked. She noted in her head that Malcolm Morgan had also mentioned these groups.

"No. I didn't ask questions. Like I said...he kept the climbing private. And I was fine with that. I figured it was a way for him to stay close to his father."

"And what about his father? Was he always a climber?"

"No. That's a funny story, actually. Bryce was invited to a birthday party when he was ten or eleven. It was at this gym where the boys all played dodge ball together. But they had one of those rock walls there. When I picked Bryce up from the party, he was halfway up the wall. And he *loved* it. He would jump on those walls whenever he saw one. Somehow, it eventually became this thing between him and his father. Mike … his father … he got some instructor to give them lessons."

"Lessons?" Mackenzie asked. "How long ago was this?"

"Oh, I don't remember. But that was Bryce … even after his father died. Even though he wasn't as enthusiastic about climbing, he was always wanting to learn. He'd read books and watch documentaries. Things like that."

"Do you know if he was seeing an instructor, even after his father died?"

"Oh, I'm not sure. If he was, I knew nothing about it."

"Do you have any idea where these climbing meet-ups took place?"

"Sorry, no."

"They're usually at bars or parks," Timbrook said. "Around here, they aren't too hard to find. There's several that take place in Jackson Hole and surrounding areas every month, so long as the weather cooperates."

Mackenzie took note of this and slowly, an idea started to pop into her mind. Rather than fixate on it and make assumptions, though, she figured she should finish questioning Janelle Evans while she could. If she was putting on such a strong facade now, it would likely break apart any day now.

"Bryce was married, correct?"

"Yes. For a few months."

"Where is his wife now?"

"I'm not sure. Her parents came into town after it happened and they went away somewhere. She … well, his wife was a wreck. Poor thing just sort of collapsed on herself."

"Does she have a sturdy alibi?"

"Yeah, she was at work. We've got at least a dozen people that can back that up."

"What about close friends? Did Bryce have many?"

Mrs. Evan shrugged and frowned—the first true sign of sadness she had shown so far. "He was quite popular in high school.

But when he decided not to leave town for college—to stay here and attend community college—he sort of changed. He didn't care about friends. I don't know why."

Mackenzie and Mrs. Evans shared a look before Mackenzie got to her feet. "Mrs. Evans, thank you so much for your time."

"We'll keep you posted if we find anything," Timbrook added.

The two women let themselves out, Mrs. Evans remaining in her chair as they exited the living room. When they were out on the porch, Mackenzie looked to the north. Although the mountains were not visible from where they currently stood, she knew they were there. She hated the cheesy feeling, but she couldn't help but feel as if they were calling to her—and not just because she had enjoyed her surprise scaling of the bottom portion of Exum Ridge earlier in the day.

"Was she that docile the first time you spoke to her?" Mackenzie asked.

"No. She was more in shock when I spoke to her. Also sort of in denial. But…yeah, I'm afraid she's going to snap soon. Bryce was her only kid, and her husband passing away just one year ago…"

"Well, I think she might have given us at least one place to start looking."

"She did?"

"Yeah. She said he was still learning new skills—that he was always learning. It makes me think that if he was still climbing, he was likely involved in some sort of class, or with an instructor."

"Maybe the one his father hired?"

"Maybe. I think that's where we need to look next. You think Petry would be willing to point us in the right direction?"

Timbrook only smirked as they neared the car. "I think you and I can handle that on our own."

CHAPTER TWELVE

T hanks to Waverly, Mackenzie had a list of potential instructors before she and Timbrook made it back to the station. All it took was a call to the Grand Teton recreational office, a quick transfer of lines, and a conversation with a very helpful man at the park. When she and Timbrook walked back into the station, Mackenzie noticed almost right away that the mood in the place was different. She tried to gauge why, exactly, but found out pretty quickly.

An older man was walking toward her, dressed in a well-preserved police uniform. The star over his left breast looked almost like some sort of stage dressing, a prop in a child's grade school play.

The sheriff, she thought.

As if to confirm this thought, she heard Timbrook groan from beside her.

"You Agent White?" he asked.

"I am," Mackenzie said. She stopped and offered her hand.

He looked at her hand for a few moments, as if he wasn't sure what it was, and then finally accepted it and shook it.

"I'm Sheriff Albert Duncan," he said. "And I'm not quite sure why you're so set on saying that there's a killer on the loose when both of these recent deaths could just as easily been simple accidents."

"I wasn't sent out here to just smile and nod and agree with the most popular theory," Mackenzie said. "I have more than enough reason to believe that these so-called accidents were plotted and planned by someone." She looked around and saw that they were drawing quite a crowd, as several other officers started to gather around. She wasn't sure if this was Duncan's intention or not. Either way, she wasn't about to fall into it.

"Would you care to share your evidence in that regard?" Duncan asked, his tone condescending.

Timbrook spoke up from behind her, apparently having spotted Waverly on the edge of the gathered crowd. "Officer Waverly, did you update the files with Agent White's notes and details?"

"I did, Sergeant."

"That's great," Mackenzie said. "Sheriff, you can have a look at all of my evidence in the newly updated files. Any questions, just come find me."

And with that, she continued on her way back toward the little office she had been using earlier with Timbrook and Waverly. When the door was closed behind them, Mackenzie took a seat, a little ashamed that it had felt so good to put the sheriff in his place.

Timbrook, meanwhile, was hiding a little smile behind her hand. "I won't even lie," she said. "I sort of love you right now."

Mackenzie couldn't deny that it felt good to have Timbrook flatter her in such a way, but she was more riled up at the attitude of the sheriff than anything. There could be all the progress and movements in the world, but at the end of the day, the older and seasoned men within the job would always look down on the smaller, often smarter, females … or so it seemed.

"Let's just look past all of that for now," Mackenzie said. "Let's get started on this list." She grabbed the old envelope she had written the names on while sitting in the passenger seat of Timbrook's car. There were only six names, one of which had a question mark by it because the man on the phone indicated that this potential instructor had recently been diagnosed with prostate cancer and hadn't been active in a year or so.

The elimination process was eerily simple. Mackenzie and Timbrook got the contact information for each of the five remaining instructors—four men and one woman. Mackenzie caught a break on her first call, to a place called Rise Up Rock Climbing. The woman who answered the phone sounded monotone and almost robotic...just the type of person Mackenzie preferred to speak to when getting this sort of information.

After giving her name, reason for calling, and badge number for identification, the monotone quality dropped out of the woman's voice.

"I'm trying to find a specific instructor," Mackenzie said. "And I need to identify them by the students they might have had. Do you have that sort of information?"

"Well, we only have our employees here at Rise Up and none of them are instructors, per se. The instructors we use come and go on a freelance basis. But we do keep records of every student they take on if the arrangement is made through Rise Up."

"Great. How long would it take you to make a match if I gave you the name of someone that might have worked with an instructor there?"

"Oh, it's all in a spreadsheet we keep. I can figure it out for you in a matter of seconds."

"Wonderful. I'm trying to find an instructor who might have worked with Bryce Evans. I don't know how long ago he would have started...but if you can prove that he took lessons in the last year or so, that would be great."

"Do you know for a fact he went through Rise Up to get an instructor?"

"No. I don't even know if he *was* using an instructor."

"Oh, I see. Well, let me pull of the spreadsheet here and see..."

Mackenzie heard the woman clacking on a keyboard, but not for very long. She was back on the phone again less than ten seconds later.

"Well, I do have a Bryce Evans here. Seems he was seeing Lance Tyree a few months ago."

"Is Lance Tyree a regular? Does Rise Up do much work with him?"

"A pretty fair amount. He's good at what he does but he has a firm personality, you know?"

"Have you had complaints about him?"

"A few, but nothing serious."

"Can you see how many other students he's had over the last few years?"

"Yeah, it looks like … fourteen over the last three years."

"By any chance would one of those students be a woman by the name of Mandy Yorke?"

"Yes, actually."

Links started clicking in Mackenzie's head as she felt a lead being formed. "How long ago?"

"Looks like lessons started last year and ended earlier this year. It looks like it was right around the same time Mr. Evans was seeing him."

Mackenzie waved to Timbrook and then pointed to the first name on the list: Lance Tyree. Seeing Mackenzie's certainty, Timbrook quickly started to wrap up her call while heading out of the room.

"Can you tell me when Mr. Tyree last worked with someone as an instructor?"

"Looks like about two weeks ago. A woman named Sarah Leinhart."

"And could I please have Mr. Tyree's contact information?"

"Of course," the woman said, though she sounded a bit hesitant. She gave his phone number and home address before Mackenzie ended the call.

As she pocketed her phone, the door to the room opened. She was expecting to see Timbrook but instead saw Sheriff Duncan. He was holding two different file folders. She saw that the label to the one on top read **Bryce Evans**.

"Can I help you, Sheriff?" she asked.

"Look … these are some great insights," he said, plopping the folders down on the table. "No one in the whole damned office pointed out this knot you noticed … the Munter hitch. And after I really looked at that indentation on the front of Bryce Evans's head … maybe you're right."

"Thanks for the acknowledgment."

"But you have to understand…we can't just shout this from the rooftops. Something like this could have a vast effect on locals, tourism, public safety."

"I'm well aware of that," Mackenzie said. "I plan to keep things as discreet as possible. It's one of the reasons I'm solo on this, I believe."

"Anyway," Duncan said, as if it hurt to say it, "you have my full support. Just let me know what you need."

"I think I'm good for now. I'd like to continue to have the assistance of Sergeant Timbrook and Officer Waverly if that's okay."

"Absolutely."

As if summoned by her name, Timbrook came back into the room. There was a flair of excitement in her eyes when she looked right past the sheriff and to Mackenzie.

"I just ran a search for Lance Tyree. He's a thirty-seven-year-old local with a record."

"What's on it?"

"Domestic violence. Two counts."

"Well then," Mackenzie said, instantly heading for the door, "let's go pay him a visit."

"Wait, hold on," Sheriff Duncan said. "Who the hell is Lance Tyree?"

"If all goes the way it seems to be pointing," Mackenzie said, "I believe he might very well be our first suspect."

The address Mackenzie had gotten from the woman at Rise Up Rock Climbing led them into Jackson Hole's downtown district. Timbrook was at the wheel, taking each turn with the confidence of a woman who knew the town inside and out. They ended up venturing down a thin side street with a series of nice-but-not-too-nice homes sprinkled here and there.

Timbrook parked in front of the address and the two women got out of the car. As they walked up the small sidewalk to Lance Tyree's front door, a depressed look seemed to slide across Timbrook's face.

"Everything okay?" Mackenzie asked.

"Yeah. It's just … this is usually a quiet part of town. It feels weird to be here while trying to solve a pair of murders."

"You know Tyree at all?"

"No. And what I saw in his record didn't ring any bells, either."

As they reached the front door, Mackenzie raised her hand to knock. Before she could, though, the sound of music greeted them. It was faint, coming from somewhere behind the house. Mackenzie realized she recognized the song, as it was something Ellington enjoyed from time to time: "Do the Evolution" by Pearl Jam.

They shared a look, and then a shrug that was almost in unison. Mackenzie ignored the door and, instead, stepped out into the yard. As she reached the edge of the house, the music grew louder. She waved Timbrook on and they walked around the side of the house to a fenced-in backyard. As they approached the small gate at the start of the fence, Mackenzie peered over and saw a man kneeling in the yard, unspooling a length of rope. As he worked at it, the music changed, switching over to something by Soundgarden. The man was lost in his own little alternative playlist while working on his ropes. It was quite clear that the ropes were lengthy climbing ropes, making it quite easy to assume that the man working on them was indeed Lance Tyree.

Mackenzie knocked very loudly on the gate, to be heard over the grungy sounds coming from the Bluetooth speaker sitting on the edge of the back porch. Tyree looked up right away. A look of surprise and confusion came over his face as he got to his feet and started walking toward the gate. He pulled his phone from his pocket, working the controls to the speaker to lower the volume as he approached the gate. He did not open it, but stopped short of the latch, looking to the women on the other side.

"Can I help you?" he asked. "Was the music too loud?"

"No you're fine," Mackenzie said, readying her badge and ID. "However, my name is Agent Mackenzie White, with the FBI. This is Sergeant Timbrook with the Jackson Hole PD. We were hoping to speak with you if you had a moment."

"Can I ask what this is about?"

"We were hoping to get some information on two climbing students you have worked with over the past few years."

Still looking rather confused, Tyree unlatched the gate and allowed them into the backyard. "I suppose this is about Mandy Yorke?"

"You heard about what happened?" Timbrook asked.

"Yeah. There were a lot of people on a few of the Facebook groups I follow talking about it. God…it's terrible, huh?"

"It is," Mackenzie said. "What can you tell us about Mandy? She doesn't have family around here and the only information we're getting is from a fairly unreliable roommate."

The ropes forgotten for now, Tyree took a seat on the edge of his back porch. "She was a sweet girl, you know? Always good for a laugh…always joking. But I got the vibe that she's sort of an introvert. She didn't like being around people. It's a trait that's pretty common among climbers."

"Was she any good at rock climbing?"

"She was. Yeah. Really agile and determined. Very gutsy, too. She'd make some moves from handhold to handhold in a blink that others might be nervous about."

"What about safety?" Mackenzie asked. She was softly baiting him, making him think they were here just to learn about Mandy. Really, though, she was studying him as he answered her questions.

"Well, in terms of my lessons, she was always very safe. But I make all of my students respect safety precautions. In terms of how she upheld that when she wasn't under my guidance, I just can't say."

"How about a guy named Bryce Evans? What can you tell me about him?"

At this, Tyree cocked his head at an angle and scrutinized her. "What about him?"

"I guess you haven't heard about him yet," Mackenzie said. "He also died of what looks to be a tragic rock-climbing accident."

"Jesus…for real?"

"Yes, for real. Do you recall working with him?"

"Yeah...him and his old man. I think his dad died a few years back. Nah...maybe sooner than that. It might just be a year or so. Pretty recent."

"Mr. Tyree, how long have you been working as a climbing instructor?"

He slowly got to his feet, removing himself from the perch on the edge of the back porch. He sensed that something was up, that this agent and cop were here for more than just random questions about former students.

"I've been at it full time for about a year and a half. Before that, I got a few hours in here and there for a few years."

"Mr. Tyree," Timbrook said, "would you care to tell us about the two counts of domestic violence on your record?"

Tyree rolled his eyes and chuckled. "Are you kidding me?"

"Not at all."

He looked to the two women and shook his head. He wore an expression that told Mackenzie he felt like the victim here—that he was trapped no matter what he said.

"Whatever," he finally said. "It's in the past. Three years behind me now. My ex-wife and I got into a drunken argument one night and I lost control of myself. I hit her twice and she reported it the next day."

"And the second time?"

He didn't appear so willing to explain himself on that particular account. Instead, he went back to work on his ropes. "Are you trying to tell me that you're eyeing me as a suspect just because of my unfortunate past?"

"No. I'm telling you that you're directly linked to both of the victims. And so far, you're the only person with such a link. The marks on your record simply made it an easier decision to come question you."

"That seems like some back-breaking detective work for sure," he said sarcastically.

Mackenzie stepped forward as his back was turned. "Why don't you tell us about that second domestic abuse charge? I can find out quite easily, you know. By making me go back and dig it up myself, you're only going to piss me off."

"I've wrestled my demons," he spat. "I don't need to revisit it."

"If you want to be cleared of our suspicion, you might want to."

He was quiet for a moment and then, almost out of nowhere, bundled up some of the rope he was tidying up and tossed it across the yard.

"It was my sister. She was over to visit me after my wife left. She got a little too personal with me—told me some truths I didn't want to hear. I punched her and broke her jaw. She later dropped charges when she heard there could be some jail time involved. I haven't spoken to her since. Now ... is there anything else you'd like for me to painfully dredge up?"

"I'd like to know how things went the last time you saw both Bryce Evans and Mandy Yorke," Mackenzie said.

"I had a session with Mandy about three months ago. She was never really a regular. She'd save up some money, I think, and then just take classes when she could. I honestly didn't see or notice anything different about her the last time I met with her."

"And what about Bryce?" Timbrook asked.

"I hadn't had any classes with him in a pretty long time. Over a year ... probably as much as *two* years."

"You're certain of that?"

"Yes."

"Do you keep receipts and things of that nature from each session?"

He again rolled his eyes, making no effort to hide his irritation. "I'm not diligent about it but if it's something you absolutely have to have for the investigation, I could probably go back and pull whatever information you need from my tax records."

"Hopefully, it won't come to that." She stared him down for a moment and saw that she had clearly gotten under his skin. But she knew right then and there that Lance Tyree was not the killer. She nodded to him and said: "Thank you for your time, Mr. Tyree."

With that, she headed back for the gate along the fence with Timbrook following behind her. It wasn't until they reached Timbrook's car that the sergeant broke the silence between them.

"You don't think it's worth taking him in?" she asked.

"I don't. Did you see how strongly he wrestled against telling us about his sister? If something like that was hard for him to divulge, causing him to get that upset, he would have showed much clearer signs of distress when we mentioned the names of the victims … if he was the killer, that is."

Timbrook smiled as she got back behind the wheel. "Where to next? If you can keep us away from the station, that would be great."

"Let's head over to the recreational center at the park," Mackenzie said. "I want to learn more about these climber groups and meet-ups. We're pretty certain Mandy Yorke visited one. And if I had to place a bet, I'd wager that Bryce Evans at least checked one or two out as well. They both seem like loners, with no problem climbing alone. I wonder if the meet-ups would have appealed to them."

"Like a place to potentially meet other climbers to work with?" Timbrook asked.

"Possibly."

That was enough for Timbrook. She pulled away from Lance Tyree's house and headed back through town. Through the buildings, Mackenzie was able to catch fleeting glimpses of the mountains and as childish as it seemed, she started to think that those large, looming shapes might be plotting to keep her in town for good—away from Ellington, her son, and any hope of solving this case.

CHAPTER THIRTEEN

The woman at the welcome desk at the Grand Teton recreational park offices turned out to be the same woman Mackenzie had spoken to on the phone. Her name was Bonnie, and she was polite, cheerful, and more than determined to do the best she could to help. There was no one currently in the office, so the three women were able to speak amongst themselves right at the desk.

"I'd like to know more about these climbing meet-ups," Mackenzie told her. "What can you tell me?"

"Well, here at the park, we organize a few every couple of weeks," Bonnie said. "But honestly, those that show up are usually pre-teen boys—usually pushed to the meetings by parents that want to get them outside and away from their video games and phones."

"So the park itself doesn't really organize meet-ups for older climbers?"

"No. The closest we come are the occasional workshop with some of our instructors. But even then, it's mostly novice climbers or those that haven't really even started to climb yet."

"But you *do* get calls from the public about how to find climbing groups?" Timbrook asked.

"That's correct. And I usually end up directing them to Facebook. Or, sometimes, there will be fliers up there on the bulletin board." She pointed to the right, where a large cork-style board was affixed to the wall. It was adorned with numerous papers, so many that most of the signs and fliers overlapped others a bit.

"Thanks," Mackenzie said, walking away from the desk and toward the board.

There was almost too much information to take in. There was information for kids' groups, sign-ups for a Keep the Park Green event, lost pet posters, Help Wanted ads, and fliers promoting the services of new climbing instructors. But then, in the middle of it all and partially buried under a flier for a live acoustic concert at a local pub, was exactly what Mackenzie had been hoping to find.

A simple blue sheet of cardstock paper, with a message written in thick black magic marker, read:

CLIMB TIME

Rock-Climbers meet-up
WHAT? - Come for Beer, Small Talk and Friends (but mostly beer)
WHERE/WHEN? - The Cavalier, every Tuesday
and Thursday evening, 6 – 8.
Bring a cool climbing story and your first drink is on the house!

"Today is Thursday," Mackenzie said, pointing to the flier.

"And it'll be six o'clock soon," Timbrook added. "You feel like going to a climber meet-up?"

The comment held more weight than Timbrook knew. With Mackenzie's suddenly resurfacing memories from her past, the idea of going to such a meeting wasn't as ridiculous as it sounded. In fact, the deeper into the case they ventured, the more insistent those memories became.

And Mackenzie wasn't sure if this was a good thing or a bad thing.

The Cavalier was a trendy little bar with twenty beers on tap—half of which were local brews—and a separate wine bar toward the back. When Mackenzie and Timbrook arrived at 6:35, there were fewer than twenty patrons. There were only two tables holding what could be considered "groups." One was a group of five people, dressed in office attire—the men dressed in button-down shirts and nice pants, the women in respectable tops and skirts. The other group was a trio of young women who looked barely old enough to drink.

Timbrook nudged Mackenzie as they looked around, pointing to the large bar. There were a few people scattered around it, but Timbrook was specifically motioning toward a pair of men sitting at the far corner. They were both drinking pitch-black beers. One of them had a long, unkempt beard. The other wore a shaved head and a Patagonia tank top.

"Is it considered stereotyping to assume they'd be climbers?" Timbrook asked.

"You know the area better than I do," Mackenzie said. "You tell me."

Timbrook did so by walking in their direction. Mackenzie let her keep the lead, knowing that locals would likely be more open to talking to a local member of law enforcement rather than someone with the federal government. She stayed a step behind Timbrook as she approached the two men.

"Are either of you here for the climbers meet-up?" she asked.

They both took a moment to take in the police uniform and then exchanged a strange look. The man in the tank top smirked and nodded. "Yeah. Is that… is that okay?"

"Of course," she said. "I was hoping to find out how these things work."

"Um … we just meet here and hang out," the other man said. "Have a few drinks, get to know one another, things like that."

"If someone was looking for a partner to climb with, would this be the right place to come?" Mackenzie asked. She got the same skeptical eye as they'd given Timbrook, so she showed her badge. She did it quickly, not wanting to draw attention to their conversation. "I'm with the FBI … Agent White."

"Ah, is this about the two deaths?" the bearded one asked.

"We're just trying to look deeper into the sorts of things that might take place at these meet-ups."

"So it *is* about the deaths?"

Timbrook hesitated, but Mackenzie stepped in. She knew that even if they did remain silent on their reason for being here, these two would likely tell their friends that the two deaths were *exactly* why a policewoman and an FBI agent had showed up. They'd make it their story, spin it, and start that local panic that Sheriff Duncan and his peons seemed to be so worried about.

"Yes, we are looking into the recent accidents," Mackenzie said. "Did either of you know them?"

"I'd heard of Mandy Yorke," the man in the tank top said. "But as far as I know, I don't think I ever met her. She did a lot of competing—like competitive climbing. Never heard an ill word about her."

"Competitive climbing is big around here?" Mackenzie asked.

"No, not really big. But it's getting bigger. You guys seen that new documentary yet? *Free Solo* it's called."

"No."

"It's about this climber…goes right up the side of El Capitan out in Yosemite with no equipment, no ropes, nothing. It caused quite a stir…and there are lots of wannabes out there trying it out now. Not the free solo climbing, but just climbing in general."

For a sickening moment, Mackenzie tried to imagine scaling something like Logan's View of Exum Rudge without any equipment. In her eyes, that would be suicide—and neither of them were as grand nor as tall as El Capitan.

"How about you?" Timbrook asked the other man. "Did you know wither of them?"

"Hell, I didn't even know their names before I heard they'd died."

"How many of these kinds of groups are around here?" Timbrook asked.

"A dozen or so, I'd guess," Tank Top said. "On a good day, we'll get six or seven to show up. We're pretty casual. Just sitting, have a few beers, and talking about what climb we want to do next."

"Do any others draw bigger crowds?" Mackenzie asked.

"I don't know. I know there's one for the older crowd. People in their forties and fifties, trying to get better at climbing before it's too late, you know?"

"Hold on, wait a second," Bearded Guy said. "You know, there is this sort of informal group of climbers. I mean, I guess it's not really much of a group. But every Saturday morning, you'll see climbers scattered here and there around some of the more popular sites. Logan's View is one of them."

"How about Exum Rudge?" Mackenzie said.

"I don't know for sure, but probably. Anyway, it's basically these climbers that don't have partners to go up with them. They sort of pair up, you know? Looking for lead climbers or just someone to spot them with ropes. I think it's mostly new climbers that haven't really made connections yet. But sometimes you'll find an experienced one in the mix."

"You've seen this?" Timbrook asked.

"Yeah, a few times."

"He's right," Tank Top said. "It's nothing that's advertised or anything. But yeah, I've witnessed it, too."

"So if someone wanted to climb but needed a partner, that would be the place to go? All climbers know about this?"

"I don't know about *all*, but I'd say anyone that keeps their eyes and ears open."

"You said Mandy Yorke was a competitive climber. Would someone like her show up to this little gathering?"

"I don't know for sure," Tank Top said. "No way to know, really. But if she was a competitive climber, there's a good chance that some of the people that show up on Saturday mornings would probably be able to tell you."

Both of the men now looked a little uneasy. The man with the beard was looking into his beer as if he had suddenly grown very uncomfortable with the conversation.

"These weren't accidents, were they?" he asked.

"That's what we're trying to find out," Mackenzie said. And with that, she thanked them both and walked away, back toward the door to the parking lot.

As she and Timbrook crossed the lot toward Timbrook's car, a thought suddenly occurred to her. If Mandy Yorke was involved in an affair with Malcolm Morgan and he had described her as something of an introvert, it seemed like one of the informal Saturday meet-ups would be just the right thing for her. There was no real connection there, no obligation to have to really open up to anyone. Suddenly, Mackenzie started to feel a strong hunch that Mandy had likely shown up to one of these Saturday morning things just based on what she knew of her personality.

"Timbrook, we got the picture of Malcolm Morgan from Mandy's phone. Do you know if anyone ever really dug deep into her phone? Or Bryce Evans's for that matter?"

"Yeah. But nothing more than what you did in order to find that picture of Morgan."

"Do you guys have a strong tech guy at the station?"

Timbrook smiled at this, nodding. "We have one guy... and tech is really is only job. He's not even an officer, really. His name is Tyler Molton. He helps with database management and security mainly. But yeah... in the past, he's helped with getting into computers and things like that."

"Call him up, would you? I'd like for him to take a look at the phones. Laptops too, if we have them."

"We *do* have Bryce Evans's laptop. But we never did find one that belonged to Mandy. Her roommate claimed she wasn't even sure she owned one."

"That's fine for now. I know it's getting late, but would your tech guy happen to be at the station?"

"No. He rarely ever is. He only comes in when he's needed."

"Well, he's needed."

Timbrook got out her phone and placed the call. As Mackenzie started out of the window, only half-listening to Timbrook's conversation, she thought about Kevin. On the East Coast, given the time difference, he'd still be at home. Ellington would have picked him up from daycare an hour ago.

Slowly, she felt that mommy-guilt she'd read so much about come creeping in. And although she knew she did not deserve to feel such a way, she could not deny the fact that her arms literally felt as if they were aching to hold her baby. It made her feel weak and vulnerable—feelings that also made her crave Ellington's touch as well.

Maybe this part of my life is over, she thought. *Maybe I'm just trying to force this part of my life to be what it was before Kevin came along. Maybe I—*

"Agent White?"

She snapped out of her wandering thoughts and looked to Timbrook. She looked at Mackenzie quizzically, as if she wanted to say something but wasn't sure if she should or not. After a moment of silence, she finally said: "You okay?"

"Yeah. There's just...some things back home."

"Oh, I see. Well, Tyler is on his way to the station right now. He should be there in about fifteen minutes. And he's all about speed. So maybe he can help us get you back home sooner rather than later."

Mackenzie gave her a forced smile, as Timbrook got back out on the road and headed back to the station. Mackenzie looked up at the darkening sky, recalling that old adage of how we are all under the same sky, regardless if it is day or night where you were currently sitting. She held on to that thought because in that moment, she felt that the sky might be the only thing connecting her to her husband and newborn son.

Chapter Fourteen

Mackenzie found herself uplifted by a bit of comic relief when they arrived back at the station. When they entered, she saw Officer Waverly sitting with a kid in a black T-shirt and baggy pants. His hair was all over the place, partially standing up in the back and hanging down over his eyes. When he saw Timbrook come in, his eyes lit up (what Mackenzie could see of them anyway), and he brushed the hair out of his face.

With the hair out of his face, Mackenzie saw that it was not some teenager as she had originally thought. The guy was at least twenty-one, maybe even a bit older. When he got up out of the seat, Waverly shook his head in mock disbelief while his back was turned.

"Agent White," Timbrook said, "I'd like for you to meet Tyler Molton."

Tyler saw the look astonishment in Mackenzie's eyes right away and shrugged. "Hey, I get it. I get that reaction all the time. You a fed?"

"Yes? And you are ... what, exactly?"

"An NSA dropout, believe it or not. I was well on my way but it got too damned stuffy. I'm not wearing a suit every day and having someone watch over my shoulder all the time, you know?"

"Tyler grew up around here," Timbrook explained, waving Mackenzie and Tyler around the bullpen area and to the back of the building.

"Yeah," Tyler said. "I had planned to move to New York and get some sort of sech security job. But my mom got sick so I moved out here again. Lined up some freelance work and decided to stay."

"He knows his stuff?" Mackenzie asked Timbrook.

Before she could answer, Tyler responded. "I'm right here. I can hear you. And yes, I know my stuff. What is it you need?"

"I need a full scan of a laptop and two iPhones. I need any contact information that might line up with our case, helping to generate some leads."

"What's the case?"

They were back in the meeting room Mackenzie had been using as a makeshift office of sorts. Timbrook closed the door behind them and filled Tyler in. He nodded along, his eyes intensely honed in on Timbrook as he listened to the details.

"So you need me to do *what* exactly?" he asked. Mackenzie knew he had followed along. He was just a little surprised, or so it seemed. Apparently, he felt that they needed him for something that he found overly simple.

"We need you to sift through the Mandy's and Bryce's phones," Mackenzie said. "We need you to check Bryce's laptop, too. Check private files, social media, contacts, e-mails, calendars, everything you can access to possibly find out if either of them regularly climbed with a partner. For Mandy Yorke, we're looking for partners other than Malcolm Morgan."

"When do you need it?" he asked, giving her a light grin. He was a cocky bastard, but Mackenzie was fine with that. If he felt he had a point to prove, he'd likely find results.

"As soon as possible."

As if on cue, Waverly came into the room. He was carrying two plastic evidence bags, once marked **Evans**, the other marked **Yorke**. Yorke's bag contained a cell phone and an iPad. Bryce Evans's contained only a laptop. Waverly set them down on the table and gave Tyler a skeptical look, and then walked back out of the room. It was pretty evident that Waverly was not a fan of Tyler Molton.

"Tyler," Timbrook said, "make yourself at home. You know where the coffee and snacks are."

"Indeed I do," he said, already reaching into Mandy Yorke's bag for the phone.

Timbrook gave a quick tilt of her head, gesturing for Mackenzie to follow her. Both women left the room, Timbrook closing the door and heading further down the hall. She stopped when they came to her office, ushering Mackenzie inside.

Timbrook's office was simple, yet quaint. It also revealed a lot about Timbrook as a person. From just the office, Mackenzie could tell many things about Sergeant Timbrook that she had not yet gotten around to asking. First of all, there were no pictures—not on the wall, not on the desk. That meant she likely had no family—no kids, anyway. This made sense, as Mackenzie had noted the lack of a wedding ring on her left hand within the first hour of having met Timbrook. The office also revealed that Timbrook was compulsively neat. Everything was in its right place, the surface of her small desk void of anything other than a laptop and a coffee mug filled with pens and markers. Even the old filing cabinets tucked in the back corner looked to be dust-free and well taken care of.

Instead of sitting down behind her desk, Timbrook crossed her arms and leaned against it. "I don't mind admitting when I need help," she said. "I've only been at this job for two years and I feel like every time something big comes along, I'm under this enormous microscope. So...all of that to say this: I'm a little over my head here. Have you ever dealt with a case like this one?"

"In terms of complexity or heights?" Mackenzie asked with a smirk.

"Both."

"Then yes...to both. And I also have experience with feeling like every move is being observed under a microscope. It goes back to even before the Scarecrow Killer case."

"Two victims..." Timbrook said, trailing off. She sighed and added: "Do you think there will be a third?"

"It's impossible to say for sure," Mackenzie said. "But since we can't find a common link between Yorke and Evans, we have to assume they were random murders. And if that's the case...then I'm fully prepared to treat the case as if there could very well be a third or fourth victim."

"Not exactly what I wanted to hear..."

"I know. But if you want to step out from under that microscope, you need to start thinking that way. Assuming the worst allows you to see past hope—something you can't afford yourself until the end of a case."

"That's pretty damned bleak."

Mackenzie nodded. It *did* sound a little defeatist when spoken out loud. But the look of understanding on Timbrook's face was proof that she had known this all along but had done her best to remain upbeat and positive. She looked for some encouraging words to follow up her little speech but was interrupted by a knock at the door before she had time.

Looking in that direction, Mackenzie was rather surprised to see Tyler. He gave a dramatic sigh and shook his head.

"I thought you had some sort of actual hard work, Sergeant," Tyler said.

"What's that supposed to mean?"

"I got a name for you. Complete with contact information."

"Already?"

Mackenzie checked her watch; exactly seven minutes had passed since Timbrook had handed over the two evidence bags to Tyler.

"Yeah. A dude named Vernon Wilcox. Looks like he manages a Facebook page for local climbing meet-ups... but not successfully. There are only like fifteen followers on there. But I found his name in the e-mails of both Yorke and Evans. Yorke had even saved his info to her contacts, but just hadn't logged it in as a name yet."

"Anything worthwhile in the e-mails?" Mackenzie asked.

"Nothing that pins the tail on the donkey, so to speak. But enough to confirm that both of them climbed with this guy. And here's one better... both Yorke and Evans had climbed with Wilcox within a week of their deaths."

Mackenzie and Yorke shared a look that was punctuated with a stirring of excitement.

"Can you print those e-mails out for me?" Timbrook asked.

"Already did. Should be at the printer right now."

Timbrook moved right away, heading for the door. Mackenzie followed behind and as she did, she thought she caught some sort of tense look between Timbrook and Tyler. The lopsided grin Tyler flashed at the sergeant made it even odder. Mackenzie bit back a little smile, fairly certain there might be something between the two.

Of course, there was no time to dwell on such trivial matters. Mackenzie marched for the front door as Timbrook took a detour for the printer at the back of the bullpen area. As she waited for Timbrook to join her, she tried to again envision what it must be like to be that high up and all of a sudden knowing that you're going to die.

And again, those old resurfaced memories came back to her, her feet dangling in the air as a paralyzing fear started to grip her. Recalling that memory did two things to her. First, it made her want to catch the bastard who would use climbing and severe heights as some sort of torturous murder device, and second, it made her not want to be here.

For about the hundredth time she wished she was back at home, holding Kevin close to her and spooling together dreams for his future. But instead, she was here, focused on death and murder.

And when the two were held together in comparison, there was no contest.

CHAPTER FIFTEEN

It was eight twenty when they arrived at Vernon Wilcox's apartment. Ironically, it was just a block away from the apartment complex they had visited to speak with Malcolm Morgan. Like Morgan's apartment, there was a decent view of the mountains and ridges from Wilcox's apartment complex.

Again, Mackenzie allowed Timbrook to take the lead. They walked to his second-floor apartment, down a well-lit hallway in a nice and expensive-looking building. Timbrook knocked on the door and as they waited for an answer, Mackenzie could see her younger self in Timbrook—which was odd, as Timbrook was at least three years older than she was. But she saw a determined woman, made even more determined by the obstacles in the workplace and, perhaps, even a desire to move on to greener pastures.

The door was opened promptly by a man who looked like he had just stepped off the cover of *Men's Health*. His white T-shirt clung to his chest and he seemed to know this. He stood absolutely bolt upright, puffing his chest out when he saw the two women standing in his doorway. That posture relaxed a bit when he saw that one of those women was wearing a police uniform.

"Vernon Wilcox?" Timbrook asked.

"That's me. What can I do for you?"

"I'm Sergeant Timbrook, and this is Agent Mackenzie White. We're looking into the recent deaths of two climbers. We were hoping to ask you a few questions."

Wilcox looked alarmed, but not frightened or guilty. He stepped aside at once and opened his door. "Of course, come on in."

He led them into a minimally decorated apartment, earth tones and whites everywhere. A large framed print of a mountain hung on the far wall opposite the television. There were also smaller framed pictures here and there, arranged in a way that kept with the apartment's tidy-looking layout. Wilcox could be seen in all of these pictures, scaling rock walls and, in one case, what looked like the side of a building.

As they settled down on Wilcox's couch, he took a small chair in the corner in what looked like a small reading nook. "I assume this is about Bryce Evans and Mandy Yorke?"

"It is. We understand that you climbed with both of them recently."

"I did. I climbed with Mandy just two days before she died. I didn't know her very well, but she seemed nice enough."

"How did you meet Mandy Yorke and Bryce Evans?" Mackenzie asked.

I met Bryce through one of the Facebook groups. He was looking for someone to climb with, but wanted to just take it easy. I messaged him and told him I'd like to if he was still interested."

"And did you know him before you reached out?"

"No."

"How about Mandy Yorke?" Timbrook asked.

"I met her a few Saturdays ago. Maybe two months back. She was at one of those haphazard meet-ups on a Saturday morning. We sort of hit it off, flirting a bit. But she wasn't interested. I think she was seeing someone or something. But she was down to do some climbing and needed a partner."

"So you climbed with her that Saturday?" Timbrook asked.

"I did. We tried to meet up several other times, but it never worked out. Not until last Sunday. We met up and climbed for a while, out near Teton Valley."

"Did she seem in good spirits?" Mackenzie asked.

"I guess so. I'll be honest, I asked her out...just to coffee or something. But she declined. She was polite about it. I asked her if she was already seeing someone and she said it was complicated."

"Do you feel that she was an accomplished climber?"

"She was much better than a beginner, but not on an expert level. She said she'd tinkered around on Exum Ridge here and there. Some of the stories she told and vocabulary she used made it clear she was legit."

"How about Bryce Evans?"

"He's a different story. I got the feeling that he really didn't even want to climb. He told me a story about how he and his dad used to climb a bit. And then his dad died. I think Bryce just wanted to climb as a way to remember his dad. He wasn't very good … sort of clumsy and not really committed at all. But a nice enough dude, I guess."

"I mean no offense," Mackenzie said, "but I'm looking around your apartment and seeing pictures of you on these massive mountains. I assume you're an accomplished climber?"

"Some would say that. I've made a few climbs most people might consider to be a little insane."

"So why were you wasting your time with novice climbers like Yorke and Evans?"

In response, Wilcox held his leg up and pointed to his ankle. "I tweaked my ankle about four months ago. Sprained it and pulled my peroneal muscle. So I was out of commission for ten weeks. I started taking these smaller climbs to start working it out once the doctor gave me the clear. And because I was a little timid about testing it out, I figured it would be safer to climb with partners. I have other accomplished climber friends that would have helped me out, but I didn't expect them to demote themselves to lame little climbs, you know?"

"Did you connect with other novice climbers during this time?" Timbrook asked.

"A few. But nothing really ever came together."

"Would you be willing to give us the names of these other climbers?"

"Sure," he said. He then gave them a skeptical look. He sat forward in his seat and eyed them both before asking: "What's going on here? These questions are making it seem like you're not viewing these deaths as accidents anymore."

"True, there have been some developments that have us looking deeper," Mackenzie said. "For instance, we have one single line of rope that appears to have been cleanly severed. With your experience, maybe you can help us here. When a climbing rope eventually breaks, I would assume that it would fray or unwind like any other rope. What have you seen in this regard?"

"Well, even one that snaps from excessive weight looks a little ragged at the ends," Wilcox said. "Even if the rope is something pretty high quality like Mammut or Black Diamond, they *can* snap or break. What exactly do you mean by *cleanly* severed?"

"It looks almost as if someone took a pair of scissors to the rope," Timbrook said. "No frayed edges, no partial wear and tear directly beneath or above the area where the rope was snapped."

"That's highly unlikely. I've never seen that before … never even heard of it. In the first place, it takes a lot for lines to break. Even a rope scrubbing against a stray outcropping of rock or something like that is going to hold up for a very long time. Any idea how old the ropes were?"

"An officer down at the station knows a bit about climbing," Timbrook said. "He claims they weren't brand new, but they didn't appear to be old, either."

"Then I'd say the rope was tampered with," Wilcox said. "Of course, I can't know that for sure. I'd have to see the rope …"

"I don't think that will be necessary," Mackenzie said. "But we do thank you for your time. Tell me, Mr. Wilcox, would you be able to provide your whereabouts over the last few days if we needed it?"

"I can actually. I got the plane ticket to prove it. I went out to Yosemite with some friends for a three-day trip. Planning out our next climb for when this damned ankle is finally at one hundred percent."

Mackenzie nodded, fully believing him. She had always been a decent reader of expressions and body language. She had no doubt that if they dug into Vernon Wilcox's Yosemite story, it would all check out.

"Mr. Wilcox," Mackenzie said, "you run your own Facebook group online, right?"

"I do, but it kinda sucks. I might be a good climber, but I'm pretty bad with Facebook and social media. I can't get the thing to kick off. Why do you ask?"

"Is there any way to pinpoint lurkers to the page? People that just sort of swing by to read what others are doing but never actively participate?"

"If there is, I don't know how to do it."

Might be something for us to have Tyler look into, she thought.

"Will you be around for the next few days?" Timbrook asked. "We may need to reach out to you again."

"Looks that way. I've got no plans for the next week or so."

Satisfied that they had learned all they could from Wilcox, Mackenzie headed for the door. Timbrook followed behind her, the look of concentration on her face making it clear that she was processing all they had just heard. Sure, there were no huge bits of information to be gleaned from the conversation with Wilcox, but it made the case a bit clearer—that her hunch that the deaths were murders rather than accidents had been further backed up.

On the way to the car, Timbrook looked at her watch and sagged her shoulders. "Look," she said. "I'm not sure how you do it at the FBI, but with no promising leads and the clock ticking past nine o'clock, I'm calling it a day. And I'm going to do it with a few drinks. You want to join?"

Mackenzie almost said no. She'd purposefully not had much to drink ever since she'd started to breastfeed Kevin; the drinks she'd had with her mother three days ago were the first she'd had in a very long time. She smiled at the thought and nodded.

"Yeah, I could go for a drink."

It was the truth, but she had a stronger urge as well. It was getting late—and would be two hours later back home. She figured it might be a bit too late to catch a glimpse of Kevin on FaceTime, but at least she'd get to see Ellington.

But she also knew that Timbrook needed the company. She was clearly agitated that the case seemed to be eluding her—and that she was grateful for Mackenzie's help. The least Mackenzie could do was have a drink with her to give her the chance to vent. After all, she had been there. She knew what it felt like.

Timbrook got back out onto the streets, not saying much. Mackenzie let the sergeant have her silence as she delved into her own, thinking of Kevin and kissing him goodnight on top of his still-soft little head.

CHAPTER SIXTEEN

Mackenzie was relieved when Timbrook selected a bar that was not as trendy or pretentious as the Cavalier had been. The bar she selected was more of a dive; only four beers on tap, two of which had the word Lite in their titles. There was an honest to God jukebox in the back of the place, playing something by Dire Straits as they walked in. They took a table tucked away in a corner, both ordering beers as a thin, tired-looking waitress came by.

"I feel like I'm missing something," Timbrook said. "I feel like it's right there in front of my face and I can't see it."

"Apparently, I don't see it, either," Mackenzie said. "So you're not alone."

"I mean, it's dealing with rock climbers. You'd think that would narrow the search down enough for this to be easy."

"Let's start with what we suspect and what we *know*," Mackenzie offered.

"I suspect Yorke and Evans were murdered. What I know is that there is sufficient evidence to warrant an investigation into their *murders*. These were not accidents."

"Not accidents... I'll agree with that one. But I see nothing remarkable about these victims. Quiet people ... no real ties to anyone shady."

"Unless there are people from these meet-ups they crossed the wrong way. And shit... I really don't feel like cross-examining every single climber in the area that has been to one of these things. I know it sounds morbid, but I almost wish there was more evidence to point to suicide ..."

"No way is it suicide. Seems very coincidental, two suicides by jumping from a high place so close together. Plus…why would Yorke go through the trouble? Evans might be an easier sell. His stuff was found at the top, his body at the bottom. But why would Mandy Yorke scale the side of Exum Ridge and then cut her own rope before reaching the top? It seems a little far-fetched."

"Well, when you explain it like that…"

The waitress brought their beers over, interrupting their flow of thought. Timbrook took hers up right away and took a large gulp. She then took a deep breath and sighed, a non-verbal cue that she was about to change the subject. As far as Mackenzie was concerned, that might be a good idea. She knew better than anyone that obsessing over a case often made it harder to view it as a problem to be solved; obsessing over it turned it into an undefeatable monster.

"I'm just going to put this out there," Timbrook said. "But every now and then, I'll catch you sort of staring off into space, thinking hard about something. You doing okay?"

Mackenzie would typically brush off such a comment, but Timbrook's observation was pretty impressive. It was disarming enough that Mackenzie found herself answering openly and honestly.

"This is my first case since having a baby," she said. "I thought this was what I needed to shake the Mommy Blues, but it's the exact opposite. There have been far too many times today where I found myself just not wanting to be here. So I'm sorry if I'm coming off that way."

"Oh, no, not at all. How old is your baby?"

"He'll be four months next week."

Timbrook pointed to the wedding ring on Mackenzie's left hand. "Is his father home watching him?"

"Yes. My husband is an agent, too. And between him and an exceptional daycare we found, our little man is well taken care of."

"That's great," Timbrook said. "Two agents married, though. How the hell does that work?"

Mackenzie took a sip of her beer and laughed under her breath. "I know. I know, it shouldn't. But we make it work. He's actually pretty great. We were partners first ... so we sort of got to know one another really well. How about you? I'm pretty good at picking up non-verbal cues and facial expressions. What's going on with you and Tyler?"

Timbrook's eyes grew wide and she nearly spit out the beer that she had just poured into her mouth. When she finally swallowed it down, she said: "My God, how the hell did you know?"

"The tension between the two of you ... and the little sly smile he gave you as we left. Plus the way everything was super casual between the two of you."

"Oh God ..."

"It's okay," she said. "I doubt anyone else picks up on it. You might want to tell him to be a little more careful, though."

"It's not what you think," Timbrook said. "Or maybe it is, I don't know. We just sort of ... have fun together. Once a week or so for a few months. But it's been a while."

"Any reason?"

"Well, he's twenty-two and I'm pushing thirty. He also has a bit of a record for all of his hacking stuff. He and I aren't exactly the best fit. And I think he was starting to get attached ... wanted more than just the physical stuff."

It was clear that she did not want to talk about it, so Mackenzie followed her lead and changed the subject. "We talked earlier about whether this guy might try to kill again," she said. "I think we have to seriously consider that. I think we need to forge ahead on these cases as if we are *expecting* it to happen."

"Meaning what?"

"Meaning that instead of solely focusing on finding a killer, we should start trying to find *anything* that will get Sheriff Duncan to fully jump onto our side, realizing these are likely murders. Once we have full support behind you, we can start getting extra security in place around high-profile climbing sites within the park. Sometimes that's all it takes to make a killer slip up ... anything to throw them off what they are expecting to be the same."

"Okay, so let's say there is going to be a third victim," Timbrook said. "Who would it be?"

"It's a good question...but because we don't have much of a profile, it's hard to say. All we can tell about his choice in victims is that so far, he's only going after average or less-than-average climbers. So that could mean that he's either going for easy targets..."

"Or that the killer isn't much of a climber, either."

"That's a good thought, too."

"I just...I don't even know where to go from here."

Honestly, Mackenzie wasn't either. But she didn't want to say such a thing out loud and feed into Timbrook's already wounded confidence.

They finished their beers up and called it a night. When they parted ways back in the station parking lot, Mackenzie thought she saw some sort of flicker of hope in Timbrook. Mackenzie knew better than just about anyone how a good venting session could often help relieve anxiety and, in some cases, even open some undiscovered doors on a case.

She just hoped there were still some unopened doors left on *this* case. If not, she wasn't sure they'd ever find an end to it.

Mackenzie used the borrowed car Timbrook had lent her from the station and headed to her hotel. It was far from the luxurious one she'd stayed in the night after meeting with her mother. But that was okay. Right now, all she wanted to do was to see her boys and get some sleep.

She didn't even bother changing into her sleeping attire before taking out her computer to FaceTime Ellington. In fact, she was barely even seated on the edge of the bed before she was sending the call.

When Ellington answered, her breath actually caught in her throat. She almost wished it was two or three months ago—that way, she could easily explain the surge of emotion that swept through her. The fact that Ellington was holding Kevin to his chest and feeding him his nighttime bottle only made it stronger.

"Hey, Momma," Ellington said. "How's it going?"

She did her best to hide the emotion in her voice. And she had to just hope Ellington could not see the tears forming in the corners of her eyes through the screen.

"Hey, guys," she said. "You holding the place together while I'm gone?"

"It's tough, but I think I've managed. Having some really good father-son bonding time."

"Keg stands, strippers, that sort of thing?"

"No. I started him off easy...just watching the Celtics lose. How's it going out there in Wyoming? Is it much of a case?"

"Yes, actually. More than the local PD is willing to admit. Except for one lone woman officer."

"Ah, I bet the two of you hit it off then, huh?"

She took the time to explain the case to Ellington, wanting to share the last few days with him but also hoping for some of his insight. It was the first case she had worked in a very long time without him by her side and it wasn't until seeing his face on the computer screen that she realized just how much it was affecting her.

And there was something else she knew was bothering her—some other reason for the surge of emotion. In her mind's eye, she saw herself suspended by the side of a rock wall, dangling by a guide rope. About eighteen feet below her, a man was on the ground, urging her to come down by herself as fear paralyzed her fourteen-year-old body.

"I think I need to tell you something," she said. "Nothing bad...just something I think I had buried so far down that I legitimately blacked it out. But this case brought it out...I think maybe it tried to come out a year or so ago on another case...with the water towers and heights..."

"Yeah? What is it? You okay?"

Mackenzie looked at Kevin, eating rather greedily and oblivious to his mother on the screen. She smiled, desperately wanting to be there with them. Seeing them right there in front of her was more than enough to push her on, to bring the events from back then to the surface of her memory in order to exorcise them.

"Right around the time Mom sort of gave up on us, I turned my attention to other things. My sister turned hers to boys...I turned mine to sports. But I was bad at sports, as you know. But I somehow got turned on to climbing. I don't really even remember how it started. I was at some park or something, and they had one of those big fake rock-climbing walls. I remember doing that and just smashing it, flying right to the top. My grandfather sort of pushed me toward it. I think he was relieved I wasn't going into something expensive like dance or varsity sports. And so I took a few lessons. I got pretty good, too. Nothing big...just these little rock faces out along nature trails."

"And you forgot about all of this?" Ellington asked, clearly shocked.

"It doesn't *feel* like I forgot. I'm telling you right now and it's all pretty clear. But I didn't even give any of it a second thought until I get here and looked down from one of the climbs. It was like a whale coming to the surface of the ocean, showing its belly. It had always been there, always big and waiting, but it had stayed in the dark. I don't know..."

"Well, to be honest, you've had a pretty traumatic past. Memories do some weird things when there's trauma involved."

Kevin stirred in his arms, done with the bottle. Kevin turned him toward the screen and his little eyes wandered, lighting up slightly when he saw Mackenzie.

"I know. But this memory...it seems fresh. And it's a hard one. The fact that I just forgot about it until recently...it sort of scares me."

"You think you need to start seeing a therapist again? I know you had a pretty good relationship with one of the doctors at the bureau for a while."

"Yeah...maybe..."

"So what was the memory?"

"Well, like I said ... the stuff about my grandfather urging me to do sports or some other sort of activity has always been there. But I remember now ... a day where I was climbing. It was a rock wall, somewhere out on a nature trail, probably out near Frederick or Able Springs, I think. There was this instructor that was showing me how to work as a lead climber, using bolts that were already in the wall. I remember he was teaching me something about crimping when something happened to his rope—or maybe it was his harness. I remember a snapping noise, something just breaking. And then he fell. We were more than twenty feet up and he was screaming in pain while I just sort of hung there. He screamed and there was blood—not a lot but enough to freeze me about twenty or twenty-five feet off the ground."

"My God, Mac ... that's terrible."

Kevin shifted in his arms as if he, too, agreed that it was indeed terrible.

"I know. I don't know how I could have forgotten it."

"Are you okay?" Ellington asked. "Do you need to come home?"

"No, I'm good. It's not affecting my work or anything. I'm just telling you because it seems like something pretty big. Something I'm going to have to deal with when I get back home."

"Want me to set the appointment up for you?"

"No. I'll do it when I get back."

"I'm going to hold you to that."

She nodded and then quickly shifted the conversation to Kevin. She spent the next five minutes or so cooing at him and assuring him how much she loved him. She hated the sound of the baby voice she used and could only imagine what it sounded like coming through Ellington's iPad.

If nothing else, it was great motivation. Seeing Kevin's little sleepy face reminded her of what was waiting back home. And now, more than ever, she was determined to wrap this case as quickly as she could—not only to catch a killer, but to get back to her family.

Chapter Seventeen

It felt good to sweat before the sun was even all the way up in the sky. There was something pure about it, something that made him feel like he had just completed some very hard work. And the gift of the sunrise in front of him made it more than worth it.

He reached the top of the trail and slowly made it out to the outcropping of rock the locals had long ago dubbed Devil's Claw. From the edge of Devil's Claw, he could see just about all of the Grand Teton ridges and rises. But the view was better than any that the park had to offer as far as he was concerned.

He stepped off of the trail and onto the large rock outcropping. He saw where dozens of people had scrawled their names and the dates of their climbs. He figured some were like him and had simply hiked the two miles or so to the top of Heinz Trail to come to Devil's Claw. After all...not everyone could be climbers. Not everyone could handle the adrenaline and the physical toll of such a climb.

The sun rose slowly, casting pinks and golds and oranges everywhere. There were early morning colors in the sky that he didn't think even had a name. Some of those colors looked like bruises, some like little slivers of exotic jewels in the sky.

The edge of Devil's Claw was only ten feet ahead of him, a granite slope that stopped and gave way to nothing more than open air and a twelve-hundred-foot drop below. He took a moment to take in the sweeping panorama but it was a fleeting moment.

He heard the grunting from below, followed by the sound of something shifting against granite.

His target would crest the edge of Devil's Claw within the next few minutes. His name was Charles Rudeke and he had been practicing for this very climb for a month or so.

He knew this because he had been watching Charles. He had been watching Charles the same way he had been watching all of the others. He knew Charles had made the rather ridiculous decision to attempt to climb the rock face to Devil's Claw, going lead solo. The fool had planned to climb the twelve hundred feet in the pre-morning darkness, with nothing but a small light attached to a sweatband on his forehead.

He knew this because he had followed Charles. He had heard fragments of conversations he'd had on the phone. He had listened in as Charles recorded notes on his voice recorder app, planning for the climb.

He wasn't quite sure why Charles was doing this. From the little bit he had gathered, Charles was in the middle of a bad break-up. Maybe a divorce. It really didn't matter, because he would be dead within ten minutes or so.

Charles was planning to make it up onto Devil's Claw in time to catch a wide shot of the scene below, highlighted in what truly was a stunning sunrise. This was another tidbit he had overheard through Charles's voice-over recordings. And if he didn't make it up within the next ten to twelve minutes, he was going to miss it.

He sat down on top of the boulder and waited.

Three minutes later, with one final gasp of breath, a hand appeared on the far left side of the boulder. He'd figured that's where Charles would come up, as the rock outcropping was heavily slanted there; it would allow Charles to basically crab-walk up onto the top rather than pulling his entire weight up and over onto the rock.

He watched as more of Charles came into view—a whole arm and then most of his upper body as he did indeed come onto the top of the rock in a crab-walking motion.

Charles looks absolutely shocked when he saw that someone else was already sitting on top of Devil's Claw. Charles grinned, surely feeling quite proud of the accomplishment he had just pulled off.

Really, it wasn't that big of a deal. Others had free soloed this climb in the last few years. It was doubtful they'd done it in the pre-dawn darkness, though.

"Good morning," he said to Charles. "That must have been one hell of a climb!"

Charles nodded. "Yeah. But man, it's worth it, huh?" he said, taking a look at the sight in front of him. As he took it all in, he started to spool up the rope he'd been using for the climb. Several of the anchors, holds, and carabiners he'd used for the lead solo climb dangled from his harness.

He let Charles take it in for a moment.

And then he sprang to his feet so fast that Charles didn't even have time to turn around.

He extended his arms and threw out a hard shove—the kind utilized on just about any elementary school playground.

Charles made a deep gasping sound, like someone trying to suck in as much air as they could before being submerged in water. He flailed his arms out as his feet desperately tried to keep their balance.

But it was useless. There simply wasn't enough of the rock left behind Charles, not enough surface to properly right himself from the shove. His eyes went wide as he stared at his attacker, trying to make sense of what had just happened.

As the open air took him, there was a moment where there was a certain knowledge that filled Charles's expression. He knew he was going to die, that the last sight he would take in was the morning sky above him.

He stood there until Charles disappeared from sight. He did not look over the edge to watch him fall. In fact, he started walking away at once, hopping down off of the rock and back onto the trail as the morning was torn apart by Charles's shrieks of terror behind him.

CHAPTER EIGHTEEN

She can't remember her instructor's name, but she knows that he is scream-ing. She looks down beyond her dangling feet and can see him clearly. There is blood coming from the side of his head and his leg is bent at an impossible angle. This is all terrible enough but even worse is the sensation of frigid fear that is quickly taking over her body.

"Mackenzie, I need you to come down."

He says this through a grunt of pain. She can tell he is trying to down-play how badly he is hurt. He does not want to alarm her. But even at four-teen, she knows that he's in some pretty serious trouble. The blood pooling around the side of his head cannot be good.

As terrified as she is, she knows she has to move. She has to scale down the wall. That part should be easy. Her line is secure and she is properly hooked to the belay device the instructor had showed her. Rappelling down twenty-five feet is a cinch, even for a beginner who knows just the basics. And her instructor had been telling her that she had a knack for it, that when she was sixteen, he might even introduce her to some of the climbers he knows that go into competitions.

She knows that his life is in her hands. She has to rappel down, has to help him in any way she can.

She begins her descent, gently swinging back to the wall to kick away and rappel down as cautiously as she can.

But then she hears something else overhead. A whining, a high-pitched kind of wail...

It's a baby.

She looks up and sees the shape of a baby overhead—not too far, perhaps a dozen feet or so. And it's not just any baby... it's her baby.

It's Kevin.

The instructor still screams from down below, no longer encouraging her to come down nice and slow to help, but demanding that she hurry, that he's going to die if she doesn't help him.

But overhead, someone is holding Kevin off the side of the cliff. He is wailing as his little feet dangle in the air. She lets out a moan, knowing she'll have to leave the instructor behind, knowing that she'll essentially be killing him.

Crying now, she looks up again. The climb is not very far at all. She could get up there on her own, without the aid of the instructor. It would take some time, but she could do it. She readjusts her harness, takes the rope in her hands, and—

And then Kevin's screams suddenly stop.

She looks up and there he is, plummeting down toward her.

She screams and reaches out, acting on pure instinct and emotion.

Her hand misses him by less than an inch.

She closes her eyes and then feels herself falling as well. She doesn't not even have time to scream before she hits the—

Mackenzie's own scream woke her up. She sat up in bed, nearly falling out of it, clutching blindly into the empty space of the motel room. Her heart felt broken for a moment as her mind was jerked awake, trying to come to terms with the fact that it had only been a dream. Mackenzie sobbed as terror and relief flooded her body in equal measure.

The bedside clock told her that it was four fifty-six. Still sobbing, she got out of bed, stumbled into the bathroom, and leaned against the sink. She took a series of deep breaths before splashing some cold water from the faucet into her face. She knew that it would probably keep her from going back to sleep, but that was fine. She didn't care. She needed to be fully awake to be able to ensure that the haze of sleep was gone, that any vestiges of that nightmare were obliterated.

If it weren't so late, she would have called Ellington. In fact, she was strongly considering it despite the time as she made her way back to the bed. She crawled back under the sheets slowly, as if she did not trust the bed. She could feel where she had sweat on the mattress and it brought back flashes of the dream.

She thought about something Ellington had told her during their FaceTime conversation. She knew that trauma from her past could easily influence the way her memory worked. It was something she had read about even as a little girl when relatives had given her faith-based books on how to cope with loss. She knew all about trauma and how it affected the brain. But Ellington had put it a very simple and well-stated way.

Memories do some weird things when there's trauma involved…

Sure, it explained away how the memories of that day on the side of a rock wall were only now surfacing, but it opened up a whole different possibility. It meant that there was no telling what other memories were buried in her subconscious. Had she really been foolish enough to think that wrapping up her father's murder case was going to magically heal her of all of her pain and trauma?

Maybe I do need to see a shrink when I get back home, she thought.

She lay in bed for a while, letting these thoughts sort themselves out in her head. At some point, she started to notice the little slants of light spilling across the end of the mattress and the opposite wall. The sun had started to rise. Somehow, she had stayed in bed after the nightmare, trying to sort of her past and how it might affect her future.

If the sun was up, she figured she might as well be, too. Maybe she'd get a head start down at the station and dig deeper into the files concerning Yorke and Evans. But first, maybe she'd find a greasy spoon–type diner in town and veg out on a huge unhealthy breakfast. If this trip had initially started with the idea of seeing her mother while living it up in a posh hotel, she figured she could still factor in a selfish moment or two.

She took her time getting dressed, again slightly uncomfortable with not having her proper bureau attire. She was equally uncomfortable with the Glock Timbrook had loaned her. But she had to make do, she supposed.

As she once again tried to get around how unorthodox this assignment was, her phone buzzed from its place on her nightstand. She practically dashed for it, thinking it might be Ellington for some reason.

But as she grabbed it up, she saw that the number contained an area code local to Jackson Hole. She answered it and heard Timbrook greeting her on the other line.

"Agent White, sorry to wake you."

"I was already awake. What is it?" It was an early-morning call; Mackenzie had gotten enough of them in her time with the bureau to know that it was almost always bad news on the other end.

"Our gut instincts were right. There's been a third victim. And this one's fresh."

CHAPTER NINETEEN

Two officers were still setting up the yellow crime scene tape when Mackenzie arrived on the scene. This crime scene was not inside Grand Teton National Park, but about three miles away from park and a bit further outside of town. Mackenzie had parked about a quarter of a mile away and found herself walking down yet another trail through the forest before she came to the site.

Timbrook greeted her, holding up the crime scene tape for Mackenzie to step through. Several yards ahead of them a body lay sprawled on the ground. Towering very far over their heads was a rock wall that gave in to assorted vegetation and trees before disappearing at an angle and then jutting back out even farther up in a series of rock formations.

"Fair warning," Timbrook said. "Don't check the body out unless you absolutely have to."

"That bad?"

"We're pretty sure he hit the wall several times on his way down." She looked up and pointed. "See how it sort of angles back? He likely hit that wall, bounced around a bit, and then finally landed here. The back of his head is caved in and there's nothing but torn skin and broken bones on his right side."

"Jesus. Who discovered him?"

"A morning jogger, passing by. She's been taken away, though. She was a mess. You just missed her by about five minutes. She said she heard screaming from somewhere overhead and then she actually heard it when he hit the ground. From the way she describes it, she was right over there when he landed, right where you came in from."

"Any ID?"

"Don't know yet. I was about to check for a wallet."

Mackenzie followed Timbrook to the body and saw just how hesitant Timbrook was to go near it. "Got extra evidence gloves?" she asked.

"No."

"Here's a pair," a male voice said from her right. It was one of the policemen who had been putting up the tape. Mackenzie was surprised to see that it was Sheriff Duncan. The other officer came up beside him, doing everything he could to not look at the body. It was Officer Waverly, looking a little sick.

Duncan handed her his gloves as if he were quite happy to be rid of them. "Thanks for sticking around for this," he said.

"Of course."

She slapped the gloves on and hunkered down by the body. Timbrook had not been exaggerating; even though she did her best to avert her eyes from the worst of the damage, there was no way to *not* see it. She only hoped the poor man had died quickly—perhaps during his first collision with the side of the wall.

"What's this site called?" she asked as she gently pushed the body onto its side, revealing the back pockets of the shorts the man was wearing.

"Well, way up there is a place called Devil's Claw. Because it's not in the park, it's pretty open to the public. No rails, no guards, nothing like that. There's Heinz Trail about a mile from where we're currently standing, and it walks all the way to the top, where it ends at a huge outcropping of rock—Devil's Claw."

"How far up?"

It was Waverly who answered, craning his neck and looking up. "I think it's somewhere around twelve hundred feet."

Mackenzie felt a wallet in the man's back pocket. She fished it out and saw that it was a minimalist wallet, with just a credit card, a license, and a money clip containing around fifty dollars. She ignored everything but the license.

"Our victim's name is Charles Rudeke. A Jackson Hole native."

She handed the wallet to Timbrook and then cautiously looked over the body for a phone. She did not find one, though she did see plenty of evidence that the man had been climbing. There was a pack slung over his shoulder, just about as torn up as his body. There were also a few carabiners and a belay device attached to the belt of his harness.

"No phone," she said.

Still looking up the side of the mountain, Waverly said, "I'd say from a fall like that, it's a very good chance he lost it on the way down."

Mackenzie stood up, also looking up. "When did the call come in?"

"Forty minutes ago," Duncan said. "We got here about fifteen minutes ago. Would have been sooner, except for the damned walk from the parking lot."

"Where's the trail to the top?" Mackenzie asked.

"Just to the left there," Timbrook said. "Heinz Trail."

"Feel like going for a walk?"

"No. But do I really have a choice?"

Mackenzie and Timbrook started up Heinz Trail less than five minutes after Mackenzie had arrived on the scene. Waverly and Duncan remained at the foot of the climb, waiting for forensics and the State PD. Birds were singing in the forest and much further off, the sounds of the city starting to come awake filtered in through the trees.

"I made this walk a few times when I was younger," Timbrook said. "It comes in at a little under two miles."

"Any secondary trails that feed of it?"

"Oh, I'm sure there are. Now that I think of it, I should maybe call Petry to see if he knows of any we could use to shorten out walk back down."

As Timbrook made the call, Mackenzie looked to the trail ahead. It looked easy enough from the start but she saw the terrain angling upwards pretty severely about a hundred yards or so ahead of them. While she wasn't exactly looking forward to the trek, she knew it was exactly the sort of exercise she needed to get back into shape. It was much more enjoyable than the gym back home anyway.

Timbrook ended her call with Petry with a sigh. "He says he isn't sure. He's going to place a call to a friend of his to see if they can be of any help."

"I don't mind the walking," Mackenzie said. "I just hate to waste the time with this death being so recent. Did you take down the name and contact information of the woman who found the body?"

"Waverly did. We already told her that we may need to reach out to her. I hated to send her away like that, but she looked like she was about to pass out. Petry was the one who took her back to her car. He just said he had to end up calling the woman's sister to pick her up. She couldn't stop shaking to drive."

"Poor woman," Mackenzie said.

Those were the last words spoken for quite a while as they started to traverse the harder parts of Heinz Trail. There were a lot of parallel tracks, walking around large outcroppings of boulders and large trees. As they neared the top, and when the trail leveled out a bit, Mackenzie started to see a spectacular view through the trees to her right. There was a bit of a drop-off made of mostly trees and fallen debris, but the open sky was easy to see through it all.

"No one even wondered if this one was an accident," Timbrook said. "When the call came in and we knew we had another climbing death ... even Duncan assumed it was a murder. Three of these in less than ten days. We no longer have the convenience of hoping it's all just a coincidence."

"That's right. It's definitely a serial. And while three deaths in ten days is terrible, it also tells us a few things."

"Like what?"

"That the killer is methodical. He doesn't want to wait. This doesn't necessarily mean he's impatient ... but it does mean that he or she feels like they have something that needs to get done. And with murders like these—having to meet the climbers at the top of their climb—that denotes a methodical mindset."

"So you think it gets easier to track a killer with every new death?"

"There's no science to it, but that *has* been my experience. Of course, I count each new death as a loss. So it's a win-lose sort of situation."

Timbrook seemed to mull over this as they neared the end of the trail. The way the trees started to essentially disappear from view, as if swallowed up by the sky, clued Mackenzie in to the fact that they were near the top—near Devil's Claw. The ground leveled out and started to bend to the right, slowly revealing a large outcropping of rock that looked as if it were some sort of bridge into the sky. As they closed the distance to it, she saw that it *did* look to be in the shape of a claw, curling upward slightly like a large talon pointing to the clouds.

"That's it," Timbrook said. "That's Devil's Claw."

"Looks pretty treacherous. Any deaths from accidental falls in the past that you know of?"

"A few years back, yeah. A ten-year-old boy fell off of it. His mother said he got too close to the edge and sort of freaked out. Poor woman said she actually felt his shirt on her fingertips when she grasped out for him."

An image of her nightmare flashed through her mind, reaching out for Kevin as he plummeted to the ground below.

Before stepping up to the rock or taking a moment to appreciate the view, Mackenzie stood her ground and looked the place over. There was disturbed soil, dirt, and pebbles almost everywhere between the end of the trail and the patch of dirt that led out to the rock outcropping that looked out to the sky.

It was difficult to tell what was old and what was recent—all except a single print right along the edge of where the rock met the dirt patch. There, a portion of a shoe print stood out fairly clear. The outline around the arch was so well defined that Mackenzie felt confident it was very recent. Certainly no older than yesterday, but likely fresher than that. She took out her cell phone and snapped a picture of it. Everything was clear from the heel to almost the halfway point of the shoe. The tread along the heel was clear, fading out as it got closer to the rock. There was a very prominent N shape that was broken up by the rock—an N that was easily recognizable as part of the New Balance logo.

"I don't recall seeing anything quite so clear in the other possible prints we've found," Timbrook said from over her shoulder.

"Same here. But I think we do have a few shots where the tread is somewhat visible. We can compare when we get back to the station."

"That's a fresh one, right?"

"Right. And it's almost *too* pressed down. It's like he was stomping down or ... or maybe he had something heavy."

"Maybe a pack on his back?" Timbrook offered.

"Possibly."

Mackenzie snapped a few more pictures of the print from different angles before pocketing her phone and stepping up onto the rock. The sweeping vista in front of her was beautiful but she was fine standing back at the base of the rock. After her nightmare and dealing with three deaths, she was not about to walk out to the edge and look down.

As she looked around on the surface of the rock outcropping for any other clues, Timbrook's phone rang. The sound was so sudden and unexpected that it made Mackenzie jump a bit. Her heart slammed in her chest, startled so close to the edge of the rock. She turned back to listen in on Timbrook's conversation but wasn't able to pick up much. What she did note, however, was a dawning look of excitement in Timbrook's eyes.

She ended the call after about thirty seconds and said: "That was Petry. We've got several pieces of information to work with. First of all, the woman who discovered the body is calm now and is not only willing to speak, but *wants* to speak."

"And second of all?"

"Charles Rudeke was recently divorced. When Waverly called to inform her of her ex-husband's death, she asked how it happened and when Waverly told her, she laughed."

"Seems a little rude," Mackenzie said.

"Also, Petry said he found out that there is a little trail off to the right side as we head back down, maybe half a mile away from here. It empties out into an old campground. He's going to meet us there in twenty minutes so we don't have to make the climb back down."

Mackenzie nodded, but her thoughts were already on the two women they would need to speak with. *An ex-wife, seemingly glad that her ex died while rock climbing,* she thought. *Sounds like an evil bitch. But she might have a reason for her laughter. Maybe she knows something about his climbing or even the people he might have once climbed with. Seems like a fairly promising lead.*

She did her best to sort through these thoughts as she and Timbrook headed back down the side of the mountain. She texted the photos of the prints to Waverly as they made their way down.

The print was fresh, and so was this latest body. For the first time since stepping onto this case, Mackenzie felt as if she were truly on the hunt.

And God, had she missed that feeling.

CHAPTER TWENTY

Tamara Rudeke still lived in the home she had once shared with Charles. It sat four miles outside of Jackson Hole, a quaint little two-story home surrounded by a yard that had started to go into disrepair. It was in the middle of a row of houses down a little side street, a quiet neighborhood with the shapes of the looming mountains sitting to the east.

Mackenzie knocked on the door, not sure what to expect. Speaking with a grieving widow so soon after a loved one's death was never easy; but then again, she had never spoken to one who had responded to the news with what Officer Waverly had referred to as gut-wrenching laughter.

Tamara opened the door fairly quickly. Her appearance did not quite match up with what Mackenzie had been expecting. The woman had clearly been crying. Yet, at the same time, the news of her ex-husband's death was apparently not going to slow down her day. It appeared as if she was getting ready for work. She held a makeup compact in her hand as she stood at the doorway and looked out at them.

"Ms. Rudeke?" Mackenzie asked.

"Yeah," she said. She eyed them both, back and forth from one to another, and then stepped aside with a sigh. "Come on in."

The front door opened directly on the living room. Tamara sat down on the couch, setting the compact on the coffee table. Even before Mackenzie and Timbrook were fully inside, Timbrook closing the door behind her, Tamara starting talking.

"I didn't even think to ask where he fell from when the other officer called me," she said.

"We believe he was scaling up to the site known as Devil's Claw," Timbrook said.

"Makes sense. He'd been talking about it for a month or so."

"Do you mind me asking how long you and Charles have been divorced?" Mackenzie asked.

"The divorce was final about four months ago. But we'd been separated for about a year before that. Charles seemed fine with the separation. But when everything was final and we actually started facing the D-word, he sort of slipped a switch."

"What sort of switch?"

"He just got very uncaring. Said some really mean shit to me all of the time. But then, within a few hours, he'd try to patch things up. Wanted to work on the marriage and try to get me back."

"Was he ever violent?"

"No. No, not Charles. The closest he's come to being violent was a few weeks ago when he tried to kiss me and I pushed him away. He pushed back for a while but then gave up."

"So he wanted to work on the marriage?" Timbrook asked.

"I honestly don't know *what* Charles wanted there near the end. He was forty-three, you know? A little late to be starting over from scratch. And I think he felt that. I think he was done with the marriage for sure—but was just scared of being alone."

"You said he had been talking about Devil's Claw for a while," Mackenzie said. "Did he climb fairly regularly?"

"Oh, he did it quite a bit when we were married. He used to go out rock climbing almost every weekend. Some people jog, others lift weights, but for Charles it was always rock climbing. He really loved it."

"Did he stop going as much when the two of you separated?" Mackenzie asked.

"Yes, actually. I think he saw the climbing as one other thing that took time away from me. That was one of the things that sort of drove us apart. He had work and this little wedding band he was in, and then the climbing. We rarely saw each other. I think when things went to hell between us, he non-verbally made the decision to stop climbing as much—as a way to show me he was willing to change without actually engaging in that awkward discussion."

"I have to ask," Mackenzie said. "The officer that called to inform you of Charles's accident said you responded with laughter. Hearty laughter, at that. Can I ask why?"

She smiled, but it was a tired one. It was an ironic sort of smile, one that held shadows of shame. "Two reasons, I guess. First, the shock of it. Sort of a *where the hell is this coming from* thing. Second...that's one of the last things I said to him. He told me he was scaling up to Devil's Claw sometime this week. But he had been saying that for a month, like I said. And I told him...Jesus. I told him to have fun falling off of the side of the mountain. I told him I'd write a charming speech for his funeral. Can you believe that?"

Both Mackenzie and Timbrook remained silent as the heaviness of this settled over the living room. After several moments, Mackenzie did her best to resume. "Would you say things were strained between the two of you?"

"Yeah. Things could get nasty. Name calling. Hurtful comments. That sort of thing. You know...sometimes several months ago, just before we were set to sign the divorce papers..."

"What is it?" Timbrook asked.

"We slipped up. Heat of the moment...it took us by surprise and we slept together. And even that was toxic. Rough, but not in a particularly good way. I think he was trying to hurt me. But he wanted it. We both did. And that's why I say I don't know what he wanted."

"Mrs. Rudeke, do you know if Charles had any regular climbing partners?"

"He didn't. I think he kind of cycled through them. He did have this one guy he used to climb with up until about two years ago. A friend from college that ended up moving to California. Ever since then, I think he's just climbed with random people from some of the local meet-ups. But mostly, he did smaller climbs by himself. Lead-soloing, I think he called it."

"Do you know if he ever made any enemies around here?" Mackenzie asked. "Particularly in the rock-climbing community?"

"In the rock-climbing community, I don't think so. If he did, he never told me about it."

"Any enemies otherwise?"

"Just me, I guess." She frowned here and looked at the floor. "I'm not quite sure how to feel here. I...I know it sounds terrible, but I hated him right there for a while. Hell, I think I still do. He was so conflicted, so needy and just suffocating. I hate that I'm not as sad as I know I should be about this..."

Mackenzie tried once again to give her some room to process it all before she moved on. This time, it was Timbrook who broke the silence.

"Do you by any chance know the names of any of these other random climbers he would climb with?"

"No. But he kept notes. He'd sometimes use a voice recorder app to do almost like a journal sort of thing...to plan climbs and things like that."

"On his phone?" Mackenzie asked.

"Yes."

"Well, we think that was lost in his fall."

"I'm pretty sure he saved it all to his iCloud account. I can access it through my computer if you need it."

"That would be fantastic," Mackenzie said. "Would you mind?"

"No, not at all. I can do it right now."

With that, Tamara walked to the back of the house and out of their sight. Mackenzie and Timbrook shared a look that spoke volumes. They both pitied the woman, as she was clearly doing her best to sort through her emotions over her sudden loss.

But there was something else there, too. Slowly, it seemed that Charles Rudeke's death was churning up bits and pieces of useful information. There was a feeling of progress in the air now—and though it was shrouded under the deaths of three people, Mackenzie would gladly take that sort of progress if it meant sparing a fourth, fifth, or even more.

Tamara came back with her laptop and pulled up her iCloud storage. She seemed to hesitate a bit as she switched from her account to Charles's; it was the first time Mackenzie had seen the woman show any signs of grief since they had arrived.

"Here we go," Tamara said. "But it looks like he'd recently cleaned it up. The last file is only from two months ago."

Mackenzie saw that there were fourteen audio files. The shortest was only forty-one seconds long. The longest was seven minutes.

"Would you allow me to transfer these files to my phone?" Mackenzie asked.

"Sure. But I don't really know how."

"I can handle that," Timbrook said.

Timbrook took a seat behind the laptop, asking Tamara for a cable to connect the laptop to a phone. As Tamara once again left them alone, Timbrook's phone rang. Again, Mackenzie could only listen in to one side of a conversation. It was brief and once again, the expression on Timbrook's face told her that this was likely a promising call. She was ending the call just as Tamara came back in with the cable.

"That was Waverly," Timbrook said. "He and Petry can confirm that the print we found up on Devil's Claw is the same as the faded one we found on Logan's View."

That's enough to confirm there had indeed been someone else present at these so-called accidents—likely the same *person. Our killer, presumably.*

"Prints?" Tamara asked. "You mean, someone was with Charles?"

"We don't know for sure," Mackenzie said. She hated to lie to the woman, but suddenly having to accept that her husband's accident might very well be a murder instead wasn't something she was ready to burden her with.

But even then, Tamara seemed to start wondering about this herself. The three women fell into silence as Timbrook transferred the audio files to Mackenzie's phone—one of which had been recorded just yesterday, providing them with perhaps the last recorded words of the latest victim.

"There's one other thing," Timbrook said the moment they got back into the car. "I just didn't want to reveal too much in front of Mrs. Rudeke."

"What is it?"

"Waverly said he spoke with a local hiking guide—someone who isn't just specialized with the park. This is a guy that knows all of the other local trails and hotspots, too. We've been trying to get in touch with him for like two days and Waverly says he finally called us back this morning—about half an hour ago. He said based on the location of Devil's Claw, there's only one single parking spot that breaks that hike up. It's the same little field where Petry picked us up this morning."

"So the killer likely used it, right? If he hiked all the way up to Devil's Claw, we would have probably seen him when you and I walked up the trail this morning, right?"

"I was thinking the same thing. The time is a little off, though. There might have been about fifteen or twenty minutes to spare— where he could have come off of the trail before we arrived. But that's a tight window. I think it's more likely that he used that field as a stop-over."

"And if he used it at that *exact* time, he *knew* Charles was going to be there. There's no way the timing was coincidence."

"Makes sense to me."

"We need to head back up there, right now," Mackenzie said. She then pulled out her phone and pulled up the audio tracks from Charles Rudeke's iCloud. "For right now, are you a fan of audiobooks?"

"Never liked them," Timbrook said. "Makes me feel like Mommy is reading me a bedtime story."

"I understand that. But maybe we can learn a thing or two from this one."

With that, she opened up the first file and played it. The voice of a dead man filled the car.

"Tim is saying he thinks he's done with climbing. So that's another one. No one really seems to be into it anymore. Or maybe they're just tired of climbing with *me*. Probably coming off as needy. The fucking separation from Tamara sucks. Harder than I thought it would be. Anyway, I found another cool little spot out near Logan's View. A bit farther away from where all of the younger climbers hang out. Took about an hour and ten minutes to get to the top. Note to self—don't piss off birds. A damned blue jay just about took my nose off this morning."

That entry ended, so Mackenzie started the next one in line. She was going in sequential order, this next entry having been recorded five weeks ago.

"I didn't even climb today. Some mother had lost her kid on one of the trails, so there was a lot of commotion. Lots of park employees and the police. It just felt sort of weird. Speaking of which, I know it sounds dumb, but I got that feeling again—that feeling like someone was watching me. Trailing me, maybe. I felt it all the way up until I got in my car to leave. Might have just been all of the commotion. Anyway, 'til next time."

Mackenzie and Timbrook shared a peculiar glance as Mackenzie played the next clip. *He felt like he was being followed,* Mackenzie noted. *Had the killer been following him? Has he been following* all *of his victims?*

"Good climbing today. Met up with Tim, up on Exum Ridge. He's seen that *Free Solo* movie and is all about trying something bigger. He wants to take some big trip out to California with this girl he's seeing. I think this is like the fifth girl this year. But he also said he'll stick it out with me as I keep doing the smaller climbs. He never came out and said it, but I think he's trying to be a good friend. He knows I'm struggling with the Tamara stuff... he doesn't want me to keep it all pent up. He also thinks I'm a shitty climber and, as he says, he doesn't want to see me fall and kill myself. It pisses me off when he talks about me like that but God knows I don't want to argue and bring out that temper."

The entry came to an end. Before starting the next one, Mackenzie replayed them all back in her head. "Any idea if the name *Tim* or any variations came up on the lists of instructors Waverly and Petry were compiling?" she asked Timbrook.

"No idea. It doesn't sound familiar, though."

Mackenzie nodded, thinking. She then pressed play and this time when the voice of recently deceased Charles Rudeke sounded out of her phone and spoke into the car, it sent a little shiver down her back to hear the voice of a dead man.

CHAPTER TWENTY ONE

It was just after noon when Timbrook pulled her car into the thin dirt parking area in the field. It had been a bumpy and jostling ride up the mountain, most of it covering a little dirt track that had never seen any kind of state maintenance. There was only one other vehicle in the field when they arrived, an SUV that had probably had a much easier time making it up the bumpy road.

Mackenzie and Timbrook got out of the car and started to cover the thin stretch of dirt. There were no markers of any kind, no posts, struts, or even rustic wooden boards on the ground to indicate where visitors should park. It made it that much harder to determine where any recent traffic might have come to a stop.

"This is sort of a mess, huh?" Timbrook asked.

"It is. But luckily, it's a small area."

Mackenzie honestly didn't even know if finding any tire tracks would help. Unless they could tie them to tracks at the other sites, it would be fruitless. And so far, no one had been able to recover any tire tracks from the other scenes.

She looked away from the dirt, to the grass and weeds that made up the remainder of the little field. The entire field was caught perfectly between two slightly rising hills. And while it did not offer much of a view, the way the surrounding trees bent outward as the mountain continued its ascent seemed to promise something spectacular above. The grass within the field was mostly weeds and thick crabgrass, trampled by years and years of adventurous feet. Because of that, it was hard to tell where any recent feet had passed through. The only clear sign of passage was the flattened area at the western rim of the field that gave way to Heinz Trail, which started about three quarters of a mile further down the side of the mountain.

Mackenzie walked over to the SUV, parked right along the edge of the tree line. She peered in through the driver's side door and saw nothing of importance: a phone charger, some loose change in the console.

"Hey, Agent White?"

She looked up and saw Timbrook on the other side of the field. She joined her, her eyes following the direction Timbrook was looking.

"That look like a little footpath to you?" Timbrook asked.

Mackenzie stepped a little closer and looked beyond the tree line. She *did* see a little path etched out in the foliage. It was barely there, but it was enough for her to consider it some sort of walkway. It was not visible from the tree line due to a thick pile of under-brush and a fallen log; it was almost as if it was been purposefully hidden by nature.

"Yeah, I'd call that a footpath," she said. "A footpath that might make it easy to come and go from this field without necessarily being seen."

Without saying another word to one another, the women walked beyond the tree line, stepping over the deadfall and onto the very uneven terrain. Once she was within the forest, Mackenzie could not *unsee* the little trail. Really, it was barely there at all, nothing more than a little pencil line that had been trod into the fallen foliage, snaking its way down a hill and then taking a shar left turn.

The ground started to swoop downward, nearly at a ninety-degree angle. Mackenzie had to hold on to nearby trees on a few occasions as the ground seemed to tilt under her feet. She looked back at Timbrook and saw that she was having some difficulty, too. The treacherous shape of the trail made it quite apparent why it seemed to be rarely used; you'd have to be very committed to what was at the other end of it to venture down it.

As the trail came to the bottom of the first hill, the trail cut hard to the right and started a slight uphill trajectory. In a few places, it seemed to disappear completely before reappearing in the form of a scant little pathway several yard further ahead. Mackenzie took note of the fact that it was now heading in the direction of Devil's Claw.

"I'm starting to feel like this might not really head anywhere," Timbrook said. "There are so many of these little offshoots that—"

"Shh," Mackenzie said, raising her hand in a stop gesture.

Timbrook fell silent, allowing Mackenzie to focus. For a moment there, she thought she had heard something. She did her best to filter out the slight sounds of the leaves rustling in the breeze overhead, of her own breathing. And there it was again—a muffled sound coming from just ahead.

It was a woman's groaning.

She looked back to Timbrook to see if she had heard it. The look on her face said it all. They nodded to one another and hurried forward, both reaching for their sidearm as they continued up the trail. As they closed in, they could both hear the woman even over the noise of their shuffling feet along the path.

The woman sounded distressed, clearly in pain. Mackenzie nearly started to yell out for the woman, but then her eyes fell on something else, slightly to her left and down another slight hill off to the side of the little path.

"What the hell is that?" Timbrook asked.

Mackenzie understood the question and although the answer was simple enough, it still made no sense. Sitting to the left of the path was a small partially dilapidated shed. The color of the wood siding alone indicated that it had been here for ages—but the condition of it also implied that it had not been used in quite some time.

As they took it in and tried to make sense of it again, the sound of the woman's groaning sounded out.

It was coming from the cabin.

And this time, there was another noise behind her complaints. It was the sound of something moving, something slight and muffled.

Again, she and Timbrook shared a look before heading down the slight slop of the hill and heading for the little shed. Sitting outside of it, Mackenzie could see a very old shovel and what looked like the rim of a tire that had long been forgotten.

Again, the woman's voice alerted. This time, it sounded more urgent, more desperate.

Mackenzie came to the front of the shed. There were no windows, only an old door that was closed, the frame barely holding it in.

She readied herself, gripped her gun tightly, and kicked the door open.

It took her about two second to gather what was happening. There were two people inside, a man towering over a woman. The woman was practically wrapped around the man, her back pressed against the far wall. Her shirt was pulled up to her shoulders and her pants were on the floor.

And then she saw the man's naked rear end.

That was all she needed to see to realize that she had just walked in on an amorous couple who had snuck away for some time alone in the woods. If that hadn't been enough to clue her in, the woman's shrieks of embarrassment would have sealed the deal. The man, meanwhile, looked angry beyond belief as he withdrew from his partner and wheeled around to their new guests, pulling his pants up as he did so.

"What the hell?" he screamed. He was about to say something else but then he saw the guns and Timbrook's police uniform.

"Sorry to barge in," Mackenzie said sarcastically. "But we're in the area on an investigation and heard a woman that was in distress."

"Did that sound like *distress* to you?" the man said, clearly still working on nothing but hormones and adrenaline.

Behind him, the woman was slipping her pants on. Her face was red with embarrassment and she would not look any of them in the eye.

"We need you to clear the area," Timbrook said. "I assume that was your SUV back up the little trail and in the field?"

"Hey, I've checked," the man said. "This isn't anyone's property. It's not private. I have just as much of a right to be here as you do."

"That's not correct," Mackenzie said, stepping into the shed. "As I said, we're here on an investigation and you're in the wrong place at the wrong time."

"This is ridiculous…"

Behind him, now fully dressed, his partner finally looked at him. "Jesus, Tim. Shut up already. It's okay."

Tim, Mackenzie thought. *The woman called him Tim…*

"How did you know about this little getaway, anyway?" Mackenzie asked, looking around the shed. The place was a dump. Anyone getting their rocks off in here had some sort of weird sexual fetishes. Or maybe they were just trying to spice things up.

"Just who are you, anyway?"

"She's an FBI agent," Timbrook said. "And I'm with the local PD. Can you just answer the question, Mr.…?"

"Wyatt. Tim Wyatt. I climb around here a lot. I do a lot of hiking. I found this place a year or so ago."

"Is this the first time the two of you have come here?"

"No," he said, though it was clear from his expression that this was not the full extent of the answer.

"Are you very familiar with the area?" Timbrook asked.

"Yes," he nearly spat. "Look…you've embarrassed us enough. Can we just get out of here?"

"Not quite yet," Mackenzie said. "You're in the vicinity of what we are considering to be a murder. A murder that occurred within the past eight hours."

The woman looked up to Mackenzie with concern on her face. "Someone else died?" she asked. "Was it another climber?"

"It was," Mackenzie said. "Right off of Devil's Claw."

"Shit," the man said.

She thought of the few audio recordings they had listened to that had come from Charles Rudeke's phone on the way back out to Heinz Trail—particularly his mention of a friend named Tim. It felt like nothing more than a coincidence but too convenient to be ignored.

"Tim, was it?" she said.

"Yeah, and?"

"Have you ever climbed with a man named Charles Rudeke?"

"A few times, yeah. He's not much of a climber, not really. But he's a good enough guy, going through a hard time. He can—wait…"

The shed fell silent. For a moment, the embarrassment of it all was forgotten. The understanding of where this was all going dawned on Tim's face. "Is he dead? Is he the one you're here investigating?"

"I'm afraid so," Timbrook said. "Tim…would you be willing to answer a few questions for us?"

"About what? I haven't even seen him for about two weeks or so."

"But he mentioned you by name in a few of his audio recordings. Recent ones, at that. Anything you might be able to tell us would be a huge help."

He looked to his lady friend and then back at Mackenzie and Timbrook. "Sure, that's fine. But maybe not here. Is that okay?"

"Sure," Mackenzie said. She could tell that he was uneasy with something. Maybe there were things he did not want his lover to hear. Or maybe he simply found himself in an odd situation, busted for having sex in this shed when a man he knew fairly well had died a few hours ago.

The four of them exited the shed and started back out onto the trail. As they left the trail behind, Mackenzie looked back behind them, watching as the little footpath wound out of sight around another bend in the sloped land.

"Any idea where that trail comes out?" she asked Tim.

"It dead ends in front of this rock wall. The wall is only about thirty feet up or so. If you get to the top of it, you come out around on the other side of Devil's Claw. From there, the Claw is only about a quarter of a mile away."

"Are there any other shortcuts to get to the end of Heinz Trail?"

"To Devil's Claw, you mean? Yeah…there's at least five of that know of. Probably more than that. Because it's not park property, you see a lot of teens coming out here to drink and do drugs."

"And have sex?" Timbrook asked.

"It's been a while since I was a teen," Tim commented in a snarky fashion. "But I appreciate the compliment."

That was the last thing said as they continued back up toward the field where they had parked. Going back up the hill that had been so dangerous to walk down was brutal, but Mackenzie managed to make it to the top, her abs on fire but her legs seeming to be okay with the effort.

Before heading back into the open field, she looked back down the way they had come. That little trail was easy to see now mainly because she had been following it for the last fifteen minutes or so, and another fifteen before that. But at first, it had been vague and had almost gone unseen.

It made her wonder how many more little winding trails like this made their way through the woods between here and Grand Teton National Park...and what types of devious people might be using them to stay hidden from prying eyes.

CHAPTER TWENTY TWO

Tim's lover was not very familiar with Charles Rudeke, nor was she well versed in the world of climbing. Therefore, she was asked to sit patiently in Tim's SUV while Mackenzie, Timbrook, and Tim stood around the back end of Timbrook's patrol car. She did so, clearly still rather embarrassed that she had been caught in such a vulnerable position, without much complaint.

"That makes three now, right?" Tim asked. "Three people dead within what... two weeks?"

"Yes," Timbrook said. "Did you know the other two? Mandy Yorke and Bryce Evans?"

"No. I had seen Mandy's name here and there, in Facebook groups and things like that, but I didn't know her."

"How did you meet Charles Rudeke?" Mackenzie asked.

"We ran into one another one day a few years back when I was scoping out a climb over at Gold Face."

"Where's that?" Mackenzie asked.

"In the park, close to Exum Ridge. I think he was planning a climb, too. We started talking and decided to do some climbing together. We climbed a few times, but it was nothing serious."

"In his audio journals, he mentions you a few times. He particularly mentioned you had something of a habit of juggling women. So please forgive me for asking, but is this woman the first you'd brought out here to your little love shack?"

"No, actually," Tim said, his tone indicating he took offense to this. "There have been two others."

"Climbers?" Timbrook asked.

"One of them. Look … really, does that matter?"

"No, it doesn't," Mackenzie admitted. "Do you think there is any chance that Charles might have known about this trail we happened upon today?"

"No. If he did, I didn't tell him about it. I tried to keep it my little secret." As he said this, he frowned. Perhaps, Mackenzie thought, he realized how scummy he was starting to sound.

"Do you know if anyone might consider Charles their enemy?" Timbrook asked. "Did he ever cross anyone?"

"Charles? No way. He was really passive. Even when it came to his marriage crumbling … he never seemed like anything bothered him. He *did* try to open up to me once or twice. I think he needed a close friend to go through his separation and divorce with. But … hell, I didn't want that sort of drama, you know?"

"How did he seem on his last climb with you?"

"A little depressed, maybe. I think he was really only there to get his mind off of what was going on with his wife. He didn't seem to really be into it."

"Does it surprise you that he climbed up to Devil's Claw?" Mackenzie asked.

"Yeah, a little. He was usually scared to climb alone. But he did make a few comments about how he wanted to try some different things. He talked about that a lot the further into the separation he and his wife got into."

"Would you consider yourself fairly knowledgeable about the local climbing scene?" She was fairly certain he would be. After all, it would be the ideal environment to pick up easily impressed women. And that was apparently what he was all about.

"I guess. Maybe a little more than the average climber."

"How long have you been at it?" Timbrook asked.

"Climbing? Maybe fifteen years. The climbs around here are sort of vanilla with the exception of a few. But they're familiar, you know?"

"Can you think of anyone you've met in these climbing circles that might be capable of sabotaging other people—to the point of potentially murdering them?"

"Not that I can think of. There is, however, this one woman. I'm going to seem like a jerk for even mentioning it, but it's the only thing coming to mind. A woman named Brittany Lutz. She's got some issues and a few of the local groups around here won't let her join."

"Why not?"

"She had an accident two years ago. Maybe a bit longer, I'm not sure. She fell about forty or fifty feet off of the side of Exum Ridge. Broke both her legs and suffered a concussion. One of her legs never really healed back right and from what I understand, she's undergone three surgeries to try to correct it. She shows up to groups and sort of gives everyone hell. She's just mean-spirited."

"Have you ever experienced her being this way?" Mackenzie asked.

"Oh yeah. Especially when there are meet-ups in bars. She doesn't come to many of them but when she does, she gets drunk as hell and bemoans the fact that she can no longer climb. One of the two times I witnessed this, she started calling everyone names. I hate to say it, but I think she just expects everyone to feel really sorry for her whenever she's around. And when she doesn't get attention or sympathy, she loses her shit."

"We've spoken to a few different people that know a bit about local climbing circles," Mackenzie said. "This is the first time I'm hearing about her."

"Well, who the hell is going to throw a slightly crippled woman under a bus?"

"The same kind that lures women to a shed in the woods to get laid, perhaps?"

Mackenzie wasn't even sure why she'd made such a lewd comment. Something about the entire situation was throwing her off and she was taking it out on Tim. Sure, maybe he was a bit of an oversexed pervert, but as far as she knew, the women were more than happy to go along with it.

"If you're going to lob insults at me like that, then I'm out of here," Tim said.

"I think that's all we need to know anyway," Mackenzie said. "Thanks for your time."

She and Timbrook watched him go. He gave them one final scrutinizing look as he got into his SUV.

"You ever hear of Brittany Lutz before?" Mackenzie asked Timbrook.

"No. But I'm sure there will be a record of her accident back at the station. If what he told us is true she'd sort of fit the profile, right?"

"Possibly. But I'm not quite ready to jump to that conclusion just yet."

But she wasn't so sure if that was true. With a third victim at their feet, she was pretty much ready to jump at any conclusion that presented itself.

CHAPTER TWENTY THREE

They arrived at the station half an hour later. As Timbrook parked the car and they headed inside, Mackenzie felt something akin to a slight depression slide over her. She looked to the mountains looming over the town and realized that she was done with them. She'd consider herself a very fortunate woman if they could wrap up this case without her having to step foot back on those fucking mountains.

"Get Waverly on research detail for Brittany Lutz," Mackenzie said. "I want to know what sort of accident she was in and if she had any marks on her record."

"On it," Timbrook said, dashing off to do just that.

As for Mackenzie, she wanted to get a better grasp on just how many little side trails existed out there in the forest. She wondered if there was anyone local who might know such a thing. Maybe a state employee or someone within the wildlife department. It would likely be easy to find someone who could help in terms of the park, but for the areas outside of the park—

Her thoughts stopped instantly when she saw the man standing at a desk with Petry. His arms were crossed and he was nodding at something Petry was saying. Then, as if he could feel her eyes on him, the man turned her way.

Even as they locked eyes, she could not believe it.

It was Ellington.

He smiled at her, excused himself from Petry, and started walking her way. As they met, she hugged him right away but then a million thoughts went cascading through her head.

"When did you get here?" she asked.

"About forty minutes ago. Some of the guys here are filling me in on the case and—"

"What about Kevin?"

"My mother is with him."

"Your mother? E, that's not cool. You can't just..."

She realized that her voice was rising and a few people were looking in their direction. She took him by the hand and tried to look past how much she enjoyed the simple feel of it. She led him to the small room she had been using as an office and closed the door behind him. For a confusing moment, she nearly lunged at him for a deep, passionate kiss. But then her frustration and fear got the better of her. Instead of kissing him, she laid into him.

"You have no reason to be here," she said.

"You looked like a ghost on that screen last night, Mac. It broke my heart. And I hated to leave Kevin, but I felt like I had to be here with you."

"Why is that?"

"Because you looked miserable. You looked washed out and tired and I thought you might want a taste of home."

"Jesus, Ellington... I've been away from you for three days. I'm a big girl. I can take care of myself. As for you... *you* should be at home with our baby. Not your mother... a woman you just recently patched things up with. What the hell were you thinking?"

"I was thinking I needed to be here with you."

She stepped back, needing to look away from him for a moment. Sure, the sentiment behind him coming out here was sweet and she loved him for it... but why did he feel the need to be her savior? How could he so flippantly leave their son with his mother?

"Does McGrath know you're here?" she asked.

"He does. He agreed that you might need the help."

"So you understand how this will make me look, right? It'll make it look like I returned to work before I was ready... that I couldn't handle this case on my own."

"Mac ... I was only doing what I thought was best for us ... or *you*. Why are you trying to make me look like an asshole here?"

"Because you took it upon yourself to swoop in and try to play the hero. You can't just do that now. We have a son ... a son depending on us. And you couldn't just stay there with him without me for more than a few days, could you?"

"That's not fair. It wasn't *me* that suddenly wanted to come across the country, was it?"

She realized she had stepped right into that trap, so she let the comment lie. Besides, he was here now. No amount of arguing was going to change that. The fact that her heart now seemed much lighter in his presence made it that much easier to recognize her anger and try setting it to the side.

"I just ... I feel blindsided. If I'm being honest, it's *beyond* good to see you. I can't even explain it. But I've been feeling torn ... wanting be home with Kevin and also wanting to be here to wrap this case, to prove I still have what it takes. The fact that you abandoned him when you could be there with him ... it's pissing me off right now."

"I didn't abandon him."

"You left him with your mother. That's close enough."

It was clear that he had not been expecting such a venomous response. He looked hurt and a little angry himself. "I'm not trying to step on your toes."

"I know that. I just ... my mind is everywhere right now. This sudden flash of memory from when I was a teenager to not knowing my place right now...."

The tears started to flow before she knew they were even coming. She wiped them away but as soon as she did, Ellington was there. He took her in his arms and she couldn't stop herself from sinking into him. Truth be told, she would not have been able to give someone a solid individual reason for the tears or the little sobs that were coming out of her throat. She supposed it boiled down to the last comment she had made.

... not knowing my place right now ...

That was exactly how she felt. She felt as if she had been split right down the middle, torn between the need to pick up right where she had left off before taking time off for her pregnancy and maternity leave and the need to be with her son. Maybe she *wasn't* quite ready to be back in the field just yet.

A knock at the door caused her to pull away. Ellington also took a step back, instantly stepping into a strictly professional mode.

"Yeah," Mackenzie said, wiping at a few stray tears.

The door opened and Timbrook poked her head in. Waverly was standing behind her, looking away the moment he saw that there might be something awkward taking place within the room. Timbrook also looked embarrassed, but she did her best to stay professional.

"We found the report on Brittany Lutz's accident," she said. "Our buddy Tim called it right. She took a fall of about thirty or forty feet. Both legs broken, one of which was left practically useless. We of course don't have files on her medical progress but that should be easy enough to get if we need it."

"Anything on her record?" Mackenzie asked.

"Yes, actually. She was arrested and spent a night in jail for hitting a man with a glass bottle in a bar parking lot. This was about seven months ago. One night in jail and then she was released. But there are two more marks in her file from where people have filed complaints on her. Two different reports say that she was aggressive and just mean-spirited. But here's the kicker … a climber reported her as potentially stalking him about two months ago."

"Stalking?"

"Yeah. He said he caught her trailing behind him, trying to stay out of sight when he was headed out to climb Devil's Claw. He told the cops he only reported it because he was pretty sure she'd done the same thing three weeks prior when he had been out near Logan's View."

"In his audio recordings, Charles Rudeke claimed he felt like someone had been following him, too."

Timbrook nodded and then looked to Ellington. "Sergeant Timbrook," she said, introducing herself.

"Special Agent Ellington."

"My partner," Mackenzie clarified. "And husband."

"Oh..."

"We need to speak to that climber before going right after Lutz," Mackenzie said. "Do you have a name?"

"And an address. Petry is on the phone, tracking him down right now."

Mackenzie headed for the door, brushing by Ellington. She was still unable to rein in the multiple emotions she currently felt toward him. Timbrook, meanwhile, walked away from the room, whether to hurry the case along or to give them their space, Mackenzie did not know.

Mackenzie stopped at the doorway and turned around to face him. "Come on," she said. "The quicker we can wrap this, the quicker we can get home and figure this out."

"Mac...I was only trying to help."

"I know," she said.

But knowing did not temper her anger. She wasn't sure *what* to feel as she caught up with Timbrook and headed for the exit. She did not bother to run to see if Ellington was following or not. She did not, in fact, bother looking in his direction until they were piling into Timbrook's car moments later.

CHAPTER TWENTY FOUR

The climber who had reported Brittany Lutz for stalking was a thirty-five-year-old man named Daniel Haskins. He worked at a small accounting firm and, being that it was nowhere near tax season, it was easy to pull him away from his work. When Mackenzie, Ellington, and Timbrook sat down in his office, Haskins looked a little alarmed. Probably because there were three of them there to question him, Mackenzie thought, once again feeling a flare-up of anger toward Ellington.

"We have you on record as stating that you believe Brittany Lutz was stalking you at one point," Mackenzie said. "Were you able to actually *see* her when she was following you? You know without a doubt it was her?"

"Without a doubt," Haskins said. "And when I spotted her, she didn't really even make too much of an effort to hide herself. She was sort of hiding along the sides of one of those little unofficial trails in the woods. I spotted her, she just stared back at me for a while, and then she casually started walking back the way she had come."

"Did you attempt to chase her down?" Timbrook asked.

"I did at first, for like five seconds. But then I thought better of it. I didn't really want to be the guy that chased down a partially crippled woman and chew her out, you know? That's why I called the cops. I figured I'd let them handle it ... maybe put a little scare in her."

"Our files say this wasn't the only time she followed you, though. Is that right?"

"Well, there was a time a few weeks before that when I sort of got the feeling that someone was in the woods, sort of sneaking around. I figured it was just teenagers goofing off or something. But then I realized that whoever it was, they were following me. The footsteps were easy to hear. I heard them going out to the climb and then on the way back down the trails to my car after I rappelled back down."

"But you never saw the person?" Ellington asked.

"No."

"Tell me what you know about Brittany Lutz," Mackenzie said. "And for just the moment, I'm going to ask that you be unfiltered. Give us an honest opinion of your own thoughts and things you might have heard from any climbing circles you're a part of."

"Well, I honestly never knew who she was until the accident. When it became clear that her left leg was likely screwed up for the rest of her life, there were a few groups that started raising money to help pay for her surgeries. From what I understand, she's never been married but it was common knowledge that she had dated two local guys—both climbers—and those relationships ended very badly."

"Do you know who the guys were?"

"No. But I do know one of them ended up moving to LA. I know this because it was a point of contention at one of the many little episodes she had at a local bar."

"Had you ever spoken to her at length prior to the stalking experience?"

"A few times, yeah. Nothing too deep, though. And it was always about climbing. She was apparently really good at it, entering into competitions and always scoring high. I think she just liked to talk about it... to sort of live vicariously through others. That's the one reason I didn't think it would be right to go off on her about following me around. She really wasn't even hurting anything. It was just... I don't know... sort of creepy."

"What can you tell us about the time she hit someone with a bottle in a parking lot?"

"I know the story, but I wasn't there when it happened. She attacked some guy in a parking lot, but from what I understand it was a guy that was sort of coming on to her. I don't know if she was going for his head and he just blocked it, but from what I understand, the guy got several stitches in his hand."

"Were you surprised to hear about it?" Timbrook asked.

"Not really. Like I said…she was known for her moodiness and temper."

"Was she ever cruel or mean to you in any way?"

"She got a little mouthy a few times but nothing serious. At the risk of sounding like a jerk, I always got the feeling that she was very good at feeling sorry for herself. She hated that others could do what she could no longer do and would try to make people feel bad about it."

Mackenzie did not want to put ideas in Haskins's head, so she restrained herself from asking if he thought she might be capable of killing people by sabotaging their climbs. She simply had to use her own logic—logic that told her that someone that envied the abilities of others and had experienced trauma because those same abilities had been taken from them might very well be capable of seeking some sort of perceived retribution.

"Thank you for your time, Mr. Haskins," Mackenzie said, getting to her feet. Ellington and Timbrook did the same, heading for the door.

"Sure. Look…I don't mean to pry, but is she in some kind of trouble? I hate to think that my stupid stalking call is going to get her nailed for something."

"We just need to talk to her about a few things," Timbrook said. "Your name doesn't even have to come up."

Haskins nodded, with a slight frown on his face. "She might not be all there, you know? There are all kinds of rumors, but people seem to think she whacked her head pretty good. She had a bad concussion but…who knows what it could have done to her head."

Mackenzie only nodded as she left Haskins's office. She was already cycling back through everything they knew about their killer so far: either an attraction or aversion to heights, singling out climbers.

It sure does seem to fit, she thought to herself.

And then, despite her uneven emotional state due to Ellington's appearance, she started to feel hopeful that they'd have their killer in custody by the end of the day.

There were times when Mackenzie realized that her job as an agent was significantly easier than it had been for agents twenty or so years before her. Part of that was the convenience of easily locating people. Sometimes it was thanks to technological breakthroughs but more often than not, she had the growing trend of people working from home to thank. This trend was the reason she was so quickly able to know where to find Brittany Lutz.

She worked out of her home as a consultant and research writer for a telecom company out of Salt Lake City. She also apparently wrote blogs and articles on a variety of climbing websites and online magazines. As Mackenzie knocked on the door of Lutz's house, she thought briefly on the instructor she had managed to save. She remembered the blood all around him, the wailing of the ambulance sirens, and the pain in his eyes. She did not know what became of him … if he had made a full recovery or if he had been forever injured in some way much like Lutz.

As she waited for Lutz to answer the door, she glanced back to Timbrook's patrol car in the small paved driveway. Ellington had elected to remain in the car, speaking to Waverly on the phone as they tried to connect Lutz's profile to any of the clues or leads they had collected so far.

While it was a worthwhile conversation to have, Mackenzie knew he was staying behind because he was starting to feel useless. He had come here to as a supportive husband (no matter how misguided his intentions might have been) and was now already starting to feel like something of a third wheel in terms of the investigation. It made her feel for him, once again forcing her to face her conflicted feelings about him suddenly being here.

Before she could latch on to that, Lutz came to the door. She opened it, stared out at both of the women on her porch, and gave them a hesitant smile. When her eyes finally took in Timbrook's uniform, the smile faltered.

"Can I help you?" she asked.

"Are you Ms. Brittany Lutz?" Mackenzie asked.

"I am."

"Ms. Lutz, I'm Agent White, with the FBI. This is Sergeant Timbrook with the local Jackson Hole PD. We'd like to ask you a few questions, if you don't mind."

"Concerning what, exactly?"

Mackenzie could tell that they were not going to be invited in warmly. With every second that passed, Lutz seemed to get a bit more defensive. She was going to have to play her cards just right, angling it as nothing more than concerned law enforcement officials before bringing the hammer down.

"Well, there have been three separate climbing-related deaths in the last two weeks, all within the area. As we've done some digging, your name came up as someone who used to climb in competitions. Your name has come up more than once, in fact."

"Then I'm sure you heard that my climbing days are over," Lutz said. "Two failed knee replacements and dead nerves in the upper thigh will do that to you." She paused here and then gave them a skeptical look—a look with a bit of venom to it, making Haskins's description of her being mean-spirited appear to be true. "What else, exactly, did you hear about me?"

"I *am* with the local PD," Timbrook said. "So yes, I am well aware of your record."

"So there are some accidents in the area and because of my record, I fit the bill to be harassed?"

"We're not here to harass you," Mackenzie asked. "We'd just like to see if you knew these recently deceased climbers or had at the very least heard about them."

This, of course, was a lie. But she knew that with her defenses all the way up, Lutz was going to be very much guarded to just about anything they asked her. In other words, she was doing nothing at all to ease Mackenzie's mind. If anything, Lutz was fitting the profile more and more with every word exchanged between them.

"I haven't been involved with climbing groups in several months," she said.

"Then why were you following Daniel Haskins around?"

Lutz recoiled from this, as if she had been slapped hard across the face. In that response, Mackenzie saw one of the emotions she had been looking for ever since Lutz had opened the door. She saw guilt. She saw *fear*.

"I wasn't *following him around*," Lutz spat.

"Do you know a man named Charles Rudeke, by any chance?" Timbrook asked.

"No."

Mackenzie wasn't sure Lutz was answering truthfully. At this point, she was answering as quickly as she could with the hopes of getting the FBI agent and local police sergeant off of her front porch.

"Would you be willing to perhaps tell us some of the reasoning behind your frequent outbursts in local bars?"

"I actually would not," Lutz said. "I am not proud of my behavior sometimes. Dealing with this injury sometimes makes me lash out. A huge part of my life was taken away from me on the day I had my accident and—you know what? No ... I don't need to tell you any of this. I'm going to kindly ask you to leave."

"But we're not done with our questions," Timbrook said. "You can either help us out here or we can have you come down to the station to answer them."

"On what grounds, might I ask?" Lutz asked.

Before either Timbrook or Mackenzie could answer that, Mackenzie heard Ellington approaching from behind. As he neared the porch steps, he said, "Agent White, can I speak with you for a moment?"

Her first reaction was pure rage. He had poked his head into her case by coming all the way across the country and leaving their son with his nutcase mother. And now he was intruding in her questioning of a suspect. Was there no end to his attempts to try saving the day?

She kept her anger in check as she tuned to him. She met him at the sidewalk, staring a hole into him as she stood in front of him. He closed the distance between them so that he could talk in a whisper.

"What is it?" she asked, practically hissing the question at him.

"Waverly said he just finished speaking to someone with forensics. We now know a lot more about those two partial shoe prints you have on file. For starters, it's a smaller shoe. No bigger than a size nine and a half or ten in a men's. It *could* be a larger women's shoe, but forensics isn't certain on that just yet. As for the heaviness of the print, they agreed with your theory that it could have been made by a hiker carrying a heavy pack on their back. But because there also seems to be a bit of drag to both of the prints..."

Mackenzie cut him off before he could finish, a new theory dawning on her.

"It could have been made by someone favoring one side of their body."

"The right side, to be exact," Ellington said. "They think there's a possibility that the prints could have been made by someone that favored their left side." He then nodded up toward the porch. "Perhaps by someone with an injury to their left leg."

That was enough for Mackenzie. She slowly made her way back up the stairs, giving Timbrook a subtle nod.

"Ms. Lutz," Mackenzie said. "We need you to come with us to the station to answer some questions."

"I ask again... based on what?"

"On suspicion in the involvement of the events that caused the death of three local climbers."

Again, that shocked look crossed her face. But Mackenzie barely saw it. Instead, she was looking at the woman's feet— more specifically, she looked at the scuffed up New Balance shoes covering them.

Chapter Twenty Five

It went easy enough at first. Lutz came with them with nothing more than a string of curses and preteen-level pouting all the way to the station. Ellington sat in the back of the car with her which, Mackenzie assumed, was why she remained so civil. Yet, the moment they arrived at the station and Mackenzie opened the rear passenger door for Lutz, it all changed very fast.

The moment Lutz was out of the car, she slammed her right foot down on Mackenzie's ankle. Mackenzie buckled but caught herself against the side of the car. When Lutz tried to make a run for it, Mackenzie reached out, grabbed her, and slammed her against the side of the car—perhaps a little too hard. It felt good but it was also a simple move that showed just how rusty her time off had made her.

Lutz cried out as Mackenzie pinned the woman's arm behind her back. She applied a pair of cuffs, officially placing her under arrest.

"Ms. Lutz, that was quite stupid," Mackenzie said. "Where were you planning to run?"

"I've done nothing wrong!"

"Except clumsily assault a federal agent," Timbrook chimed in.

Ellington joined them, instantly going to Mackenzie's side. She could tell it was killing him to not be able to check her over. It had been a simple kick, nothing serious, but she could see that look of concern on his face. It was a look she'd seen a lot during her pregnancy and delivery—the look of a man who was diligent about making sure his wife was well taken care of.

Timbrook took the lead as they headed into the station, Mackenzie behind her as she ushered Lutz inside. Ellington brought up the rear and even then, Mackenzie could feel his concern or her, like the heat of off a stove burner that has just been turned off.

The trio split up when they entered the station. Mackenzie led Lutz directly to the small interrogation room at the back of the building while Timbrook and Ellington met with Waverly to get printouts of the forensic files.

Inside the interrogation room, Mackenzie gave Lutz a little push toward the table. A chair sat on either side of it, but Lutz did not take one. Instead, she turned her full attention to Mackenzie, her sneer one of the sharpest Mackenzie had ever seen.

"Do you enjoy pushing around crippled people?" she asked.

"I don't, actually. And by the way, you didn't seem too crippled out in the parking lot when you took that kick at me."

"You have no right to have me here."

"Maybe you're right. Hopefully we'll find out soon enough."

Behind Mackenzie, Ellington and Timbrook entered the room. Timbrook was looking over one of the printouts from Waverly's files. She handed it to Mackenzie as she finished it up.

"What's that?" Lutz asked. She sounded on edge ... nervous.

Mackenzie scanned the paper, detailing the findings from the shoe prints. There was nothing other than what Ellington had already told her, but seeing it in writing was somehow much more damning.

"How old are the shoes you're wearing?" Mackenzie asked.

"What?"

"How old are those shoes?"

"I don't know. A year or so."

"Is that the kind of shoe you used to wear when you went climbing?"

"No. Apparently, you know jack shit about climbing. These are not good shoes for that. I use these for hiking."

"You can do that on your bad knee?" Timbrook asked.

"Yes. The doctors have been on me to exercise it more."

"What exactly caused your accident?" Mackenzie asked.

Lutz shook her head, fuming now. "I'm not answering any more of your questions. Not until I get a lawyer in here."

"Fine. What I do need from you is one of your shoes."

"Why are you so fucking obsessed with my shoes?" Lutz was livid now. Her eyes were wide and she was trembling with rage. Mackenzie thought she might be getting a glimpse of the version of Lutz that had made so many appearances in bars.

"We need to compare them with prints found at a crime scene."

Lutz actually laughed at this, slapping her cuffed hands on the table in front of her. She immediately started to kick off her shoes under the table, still laughing the entire time. Using her right foot, she literally kicked one of the shoes out to them, striking Timbrook on the leg. Timbrook picked it up and looked at the bottom. Her face went slack for a moment and she then showed it to Mackenzie.

It was a match.

Or, at least, it appeared to be. Even the better of the two prints they had to work with wasn't completely clear. But there was more than enough visible to show that the bottoms of both shoes were pretty much identical.

Slowly, Timbrook walked over to Lutz. She knelt down directly beside the woman and did her best to lock eyes with her. "Ms. Lutz…when was the last time you were out for a hike?"

"Two days ago."

In Mackenzie's mind, another link fell into place. *We got her,* she thought.

"And where did you go hiking?" Timbrook asked.

Lutz shook her head and started to laugh again. This time, it was more like a cackle. Something about the sound of it caused Mackenzie's guard to go up a bit. When she looked to the woman, it only made it worse. There was something in Lutz's eyes that looked hazy and distant. It was a look she had seen a few times before in the faces of people that weren't all there—people that had some sort of detachment from reality.

"Answer me, Ms. Lutz," Timbrook said.

"Timbrook..."

But Mackenzie's warning came about two seconds too late.

Mid-cackle, Lutz drove her head forward. A sick *thud* filled the room for a moment. Timbrook groaned out as she fell backward, grasping at her face. Lutz fell partially forward on the table, like a bored kid at school, howling and laughing all at once.

Mackenzie dashed for Timbrook while Ellington handled Lutz. Timbrook was getting back to her feet, using the wall for support. Her hand cupped the lower hand of her face but Mackenzie could already see the blood.

"Where the hell did that come from?" Timbrook breathed through her hand and the blood.

"Quiet," Mackenzie instructed her. "You sit down and tilt your head back."

Timbrook did exactly that as Mackenzie knelt down beside her. Meanwhile, Lutz was still laughing, now suppressed to giggles. Ellington had her on her feet and pressed against the far wall.

"Got a holding cell in this place?" he asked Timbrook.

"Take her out to Waverly or Petry. They'll handle it."

"No talking," Mackenzie said as she slowly removed Timbrook's hand.

The blood was coming from her nose. The slight skew along the lower bridge told her that Timbrook's nose was broken.

"You dizzy?" Mackenzie asked.

Timbrook shook her head. "It's broken, huh?"

"Yeah, she got you pretty good."

"But we got her, too, right? It's her..."

Mackenzie was hesitant to say anything at first. But then she saw the blood on Timbrook's face and the sheet of paper with the photo of the shoe print from Devil's Claw.

"Yeah," she finally said. "I think it just might be. I think we got our killer."

❧   ❧   ❧

While Timbrook was taken to the hospital to get her nose tended to, Mackenzie and Ellington sat in the little conference room where she had been doing her best to help tie this case up for the last few days. Ellington still looked distracted and out of sorts. This bothered Mackenzie, but not more than the feeling that she and Timbrook may have just unknowingly crossed a line. And it was a line that she *should* have seen.

"What's on your mind?" Ellington asked.

"Brittany Lutz's medical records. We know she had a concussion. But I want to know how bad. I want to know if she could have suffered some other kind of brain-related trauma. There near the end, right before she headbutted Timbrook…"

"Yeah, I saw. And those laughs."

"If she *is* the killer and it turns out that she's got some sort of mental condition because of that accident, she'll likely walk. And the local PD—and us, as well—could be in a lot of trouble."

"You think it's her?"

"It makes sense. I mean, the pieces all add up, right down to those shoe prints. This new question mark of whether or not she might have some sort of mental detachment makes it seem even more likely. But there's something about it all that just sort of feels off. And I don't know what it is."

She grabbed the papers in front of her and looked at them. She then held up her phone, opening up a picture she had taken of Lutz's shoe after she had been placed in the holding cell. The pattern was the same, as was the size and placement of the New Balance logo, half of which was partially cut off in the print. After much studying and staring, that much was clear. She studied the edges right where the heel and arch met. There *could* be some discrepancy there, but it was too hard to tell because of the dragging of the foot.

Dragging because she was favoring that side, she thought. *Even the impact of the footprint tells you it was Lutz. Why are you making this harder than it has to be?*

She knew why. It was because there was something that felt wrong about it all. And even though she did not yet know what it was, it was a feeling that had proven useful in the past.

"Hey, Mac?"

"Yeah?"

"I love you. I'm sorry if I screwed things up by coming out here to be with you. In hindsight, it wasn't the best call. I think I felt it on the plane over here. But this whole being apart thing is new to me, too. And it's harder now that we have a kid, you know?"

He reached out across the table for her hand. She let him take it. She had not even stopped to consider how her going back to work might affect him—especially on a case that he was not involved in.

"I miss him," Ellington said. "After just a day, I miss him. Is that nuts?"

"No. I do, too. So much that it hurts."

She gave his hand a squeeze and got to her feet. She looked out the window and saw dusk approaching. "Come on," she said. "I want to grab a bite to eat and check in on Timbrook."

As they got to their feet and started for the door, Sheriff Duncan stepped into the frame. He looked as if he were in a hurry, his face a little red and his eyes bewildered. But when he looked at Mackenzie, he smiled.

"Damn good work, Agent White. I do apologize if I seemed stubborn at the start."

"Hey, what matters is that it looks like we got our killer."

"Timbrook's broken nose seems worth the sacrifice, huh?"

She bit back the first comment that came to mind. Instead, she said: "Timbrook is an amazing officer. Her insights are sharp and, at the risk of seeming arrogant, she's taking a lot of subtle and not-so-subtle grief from most of the men here. Let her do her thing, Sheriff. She's going to do some great things if you let her."

Duncan looked to the floor, nodded, and then hurried on his way.

"You want to get out of here?" Ellington said.

"Yeah, let's do that. Dinner, Timbrook, and then home. To Kevin."

"Well, I already checked on flights out of here. The soonest one without several connecting flights isn't until eight o'clock in the morning."

She surprised herself when she leaned over and kissed him. It was a brief but passionate one and in it, she was reminded of how warm he was—of how caring of a man he could be. And because of that, it almost made sense that he had come out here to her. She wondered if she had been too hard on him.

"Then I guess we'll have to spend the night in my motel room."

"That sounds kind of great."

They left the conference room and headed for the exit, hand in hand. But even then, Mackenzie was not able to consider the case closed or to tell herself she had finished a job well done. Something nagged at her in the back of her mind, something that made her wonder if the partially crippled woman in the holding cell would even be capable of killing.

That nagging feeling followed her out into the late afternoon and did not let go.

CHAPTER TWENTY SIX

Crickets and some kind of tree frog was all he could hear. His own footsteps seemed to get drowned out by his own anticipation—his own desires. As he stepped up to the base of the rock wall, he felt like he might very well be the only person on the planet. He reached out and touched the rock. It was warm under his hand, despite the cooler temperature of the night.

He realized that this was risky. Less than twenty hours ago, the police had been here, looking down at the body of Charles Rudeke. The body, of course, had been removed, but there were still some slight signs of his body having been there, as well as the passing feet of the police.

He still could not believe he was a murderer. More than that, he could not believe how natural it felt. It had been hard the first time—cutting Mandy Yorke's line and then watching her fall. At least then he had not touched anyone. He had only snipped a line and then hid to watch the results.

But with Bryce Evans and then Charlie Rudeke, it had been different. He'd been more intentional. He had touched them, had made it a more deeply connected event. Their deaths had not been as passive as cutting a rope. He had laid hands on them. He had killed them, plain and simple.

And it had felt good. It *still* felt good. He wasn't sure why. He honestly wasn't even sure why he was doing these things in the first place.

At first, he'd thought it was envy. But it was something more, something he could not put a name to. He did not feel that these people deserved to die. They had done nothing to him, after all. But they *had* to die. If he was ever going to move on with his life and get over his own fears, he knew he'd have to do some drastic things.

The alarming thing was that now, even after having killed three people, the act of murder did not feel drastic to him.

He looked up the face of the rock wall. The moonlight made it look like some sort of massive tomb or gravestone. He smiled, placing his hands in a slight crevasse and remembering what it had been like not too long ago—climbing, off of the ground and in the air with life and death balance above and below him. He looked up and imagine himself climbing. He imagined himself up there with no ropes, no harness. Just his hands, his heart, his bravery.

But even the thought sent a spike of fear through him. He shuddered. It made him feel weak and insignificant. It made him feel an anger that he had never quite learned how to express properly.

But he was learning. And soon, he'd find a way around it.

Even if it took a fourth, fifth, or sixth murder, he'd rule over his fear and find a way to start climbing again.

And he thought he knew exactly where to continue.

CHAPTER TWENTY SEVEN

By the time Mackenzie and Ellington showed up at the hospital, Timbrook was already checking out. She was signing the last of her paperwork on the visitor side of a row of glass partitions in the central lobby when the agents found her. She was signing with one hand and holding an ice pack to her nose with the other. She gave a half-hearted smile when she saw them approaching.

"What's the verdict?" Mackenzie asked.

Timbrook slid the paperwork over to a woman behind a glass partition, turned to them, and sighed. "She broke it. Luckily, it won't require surgery. The docs realigned it and I just need to keep it iced. I won't lie, though ... it hurts like a bitch."

"Do you need a ride home?"

"No." She then grinned sheepishly and added: "Tyler is on his way to pick me up."

"We'll get out of your hair, then," Mackenzie said.

"You're fine. Look ... I'm glad you came by. I wanted you to know how much of a pleasure it was to work with you these last few days."

"The pleasure was all mine."

"Thanks for the sentiment, but I know you're dealing with a lot back home. I hope I was of some help in wrapping this case."

"You were. And I made no secret about how well you did. I might have put a little something in Duncan's ear."

"Are you by any chance a hugger?"

Mackenzie shrugged while Ellington chuckled. "She is not much of a hugger."

"But I make exceptions," Mackenzie said. She then stepped in and gave Timbrook a brief, friendly hug. "Keep up the good work, Sergeant Timbrook."

They broke the hug and Mackenzie realized that she was more eager than ever to get back home. When she thought of Kevin with Ellington's mother she *did* get upset, but she knew she needed to let that go for now. She was learning that she and Ellington had a lot of things to work on now that they were parents.

As if on cue, she spotted a child as she and Ellington headed for the exit doors. It was a little girl, sitting next to her mother. The little girl was working on the craft of tying her shoes, along with the assistance of a tired-looking mother. The girl's shoes featured one of the ponies from *My Little Pony*, both on the sides and on the bottom. It was an extremely tacky shoe, so tacky that for a moment, it was all Mackenzie could think about.

She focused on the sole of the girl's shoe, complete with the slightly embossed face of a pony. It was unique-looking, that was for sure. But it also made her think of a rather un-unique shoe that she had been focusing on for the past several hours. Habitually, she started to glance around the waiting room, taking note of the shoes on everyone's feet. Most wore sneakers, though there were a few Croc-style slip-ons and even one woman in a pair of high heels. But in terms of the sneakers, she was surprised to see how similar they all were. She saw familiar brands, including several pairs of New Balance, which of course brought Brittany Lutz's shoes to mind.

"Mac, you okay?" Ellington asked.

"Yeah," she answered as they reached the automatic doors and walked through them.

"I know that look. You're not completely happy with the way this all turned out, are you?"

"I don't know yet."

"You think grabbing dinner might help?"

She nodded, though her mind was elsewhere. She was thinking of shoes, but more importantly, she was thinking of how a woman with a permanently damaged knee might make it up and down the same trails that she herself had struggled with. She then considered the faded and dragged edges of the footprints they had been studying from the case and slowly, Mackenzie was able to place a name to that feeling that had been nagging her since placing Lutz in a holding cell.

That nagging feeling was doubt.

There was a tepid feeling in the air between them as they settled down into the hotel for the night. It was an unspoken agreement they could both feel—that there would be no sexual reconciliation between them. Typically, Mackenzie was the aggressor in the physical aspects of their relationship and though she was up for it physically, she could not get there emotionally. It was yet another clue that they had some things to work on.

Mackenzie was not at all surprised that she found it difficult to fall asleep. While it felt incredibly good to have Ellington there after three nights without him, her mind was simply scattered everywhere else. She wondered how Kevin was doing with Ellington's mother. She wondered how Sheriff Duncan and the rest of his force were handling the sudden arrest of Brittany Lutz as the primary suspect of the three recent murders.

But she was also thinking about shoes and the sort of mindset it took for someone to get a thrill out of climbing mountains. She felt that she could identify with it because, as her recent resurfaced memories were showing, she had once dabbled in it. And as she lay awake, staring into the darkness, she started to understand that her doubt came from that place. She felt that she was starting to misunderstand the mentality of climbers.

Once the pieces had all started to fall into place and the ending of the case looked to be right on the horizon, she had allowed herself to assume that the killer was likely striking out of jealousy or envy. She supposed that could be fundamentally true, but something about it did not seem to make sense. Climbing a mountain or a simple rock face—even the act of coming to the top of a climb and peering off of some high precipice like Devil's Claw—wasn't just about bravery and skill.

It also came down to adrenaline and an absence of fear that the majority to rational-thinking humans tended to cling to. It made her think that the killer might not have been killing out of jealousy at all. Maybe there was some other reason.

When she rolled over and saw that it was two oh-four in the morning, she realized that sleep might not even come at all. She'd been hoping to fall asleep quickly, to get back home as fast as possible and take Kevin up into her arms. But here she was, obsessing over a case that anyone else would likely have considered closed.

But she couldn't get there yet. Truth be told, the more she thought about it, the more she started to think that Brittany Lutz did not deserve the holding cell she was currently in. If anything, she needed some sort of psychological help.

Mackenzie quietly got out of bed and grabbed up her phone. Not wanting to wake Ellington and not having her earbuds packed, she went into the bathroom and sat on the closed toilet. She pulled up Charles Rudeke's audio files and started to listen to them again. She had only a slight idea of what she was looking for and, quite honestly, wasn't even sure she would find it.

She listened to the file where he spoke about the feeling of being followed. Mackenzie wondered if this might have been Brittany Lutz, again stalking after another climber. Or perhaps Brittany Lutz was a special case; maybe she had only followed Charles.

But why? There's no obvious connection between the two...

This train of thought was derailed when she came to the sixth recording, one dated just over five weeks ago. When she realized the depth of the entry, she started it over and played it back from the start. She listened intently as Charles Rudeke's voice filled the bathroom.

"Tamara never understood why I do this. And I wish I could explain it to her. I wish I could tell her how it feels like I'm conquering something, even on the smaller climbs. I know she views it as nothing more than a grown man sidestepping into childlike adventures. She thinks it's immature. She's never come out and said it, but I think that's the case.

"I started mapping out the route to the top of Devil's Claw today. I think it's going to be relatively easy. I'm going up on the side no one else has really ever done before. The start of it is down this weird little path that arcs right back up on the eastern side of the rock face. It'll probably add an extra twenty minutes to the climb, but there's plenty of natural handholds along the way. Some guys at the bar were saying the climb on this side is a little harder, but I don't see it. I think it'll go well. Just need to practice the switch-over halfway up and work on getting back on track with my fingerboard training.

"This might be the last time I attempt to get Tamara interested in this. A few of the guys I've met at the meet-ups talk about how their wives and girlfriends are turned on by the fact that they climb. Tamara needs to hang with some of these women. I don't know what her deal is. I wish I could explain to her the adrenaline rush, the sense of clarity... the realization that I've just done something that not everyone can do. I used to be one of those beginners that froze up ten feet off the ground and never made it back to climbing. To think of how far I've come and not being able to really share that with her... it sucks."

Mackenzie stopped the recording and thought about the last few comments.

... the realization that I've just done something that not everyone can do...

... those beginners that froze up ten feet off the ground and never made it back to climbing...

Brittany Lutz had seemed like a strong suspect because she had been injured and something she loved had been taken away from her. Add a potential head injury, and she seemed to be a good fit. But still, the issue of her injured leg needed to be considered. And even if she had been stalking Charles Rudeke and other climbers, there was no evidence that she had done so higher up on tougher trails or at the peaks of higher climbs.

She went back out into the room and grabbed the case file. She glanced to the bedside clock, which read two thirty-seven, and then at Ellington. She kissed him softly on the forehead and then tore off a sheet of paper from the notepad on the bedside table. She scrawled a quick note—*At the station*—and set it on her side of the bed.

She walked back out into the night, toward the department car she had been fully prepared to return to the station in the morning. But as she got back behind the wheel, she had sinking feeling that she and Ellington might miss their flight in the morning, But that was secondary in that moment. Instead, she was thinking of climbers just starting out, climbers who realized several feet up that they feared the act far too much to go through with it.

She thought of someone so certain of themselves, suddenly paralyzed by fear, and what that must feel like.

By the time she was halfway to the station, this started to make a great deal of sense to her. And she started to think that Brittany Lutz was not the killer at all.

CHAPTER TWENTY EIGHT

The station was quiet when Mackenzie got there. There was a small woman sitting at the dispatch desk and two policemen she had not yet met sitting at desks, going over files and casework. Mackenzie knew that at least three other officers would be out on patrol. It made her wonder if there was any officer on duty to manage the confinement and needs of Brittany Lutz.

Mackenzie took her case files to the back of the building to set up shop in the makeshift office she had been using. When she got there, she was surprised to see the door open and the light on. When she entered, she saw Timbrook sitting at the table. She was poring over a few files, one of which was a copy of the shoe print photos from Logan's View and Devil's Claw.

She looked up when Mackenzie entered the room. Surprisingly, she did not looked tired. If anything, she looked embarrassed to have been caught working at such an hour. Her nose was severely bruised from Lutz's attack but the doctors had set it back quite nicely.

"Burning the midnight oil?" Mackenzie asked as she sat down at the table.

"Yeah, I couldn't sleep."

"I thought you were going to Tyler's."

"I did. I didn't want to keep him up, so I came down here. I thought about going to speak with Lutz, but thought better of it. I'm still a little pissed about my nose."

"I think we should stay away from her until she can undergo a psych evaluation anyway," Mackenzie said. "So, what exactly are you looking for right now?"

"I don't know. Something just feels sort of off. I feel like we missed something."

"That's why I'm here."

"What have you got?" Timbrook asked.

Mackenzie spent the next few minutes explaining how she was starting to think that the shoes matching up could be a coincidence. Until someone could take Lutz's shoe to the sites and place them side by side, there was no way to be absolutely sure they were a perfect match in size. She then explained how she was starting to think the methods and victim selection of the killer were not the work of someone using envy as a platform, but fear—perhaps a fear of heights and climbing that could have *turned into* envy, but not an organic form of it. She ended with her speculation that even though Lutz admitted that she enjoyed hiking, they had no proof that her bum knee allowed her to take the more adventurous avenues that would lead to places like the top of Devil's Claw.

"About the shoes," Timbrook said. "Waverly left me a little note in the files sometime after my nose got broken. He said he did some digging and found out that the design on the bottom of the shoe print at those two sites probably is the same as the ones on Lutz's shoes. But what he also found is that this particular pattern is found on the bottom of three different shoe designs put out by New Balance—and two of them were the most popular sellers for the company within the last year. Which means that even if they *are* an exact match, it's not as significant as we thought."

"So let's say we start from scratch on this," Mackenzie said. "If we assume that this new profile is the right one, where would we start to look?"

She had a few ideas of her own, but she wanted to give Timbrook this opportunity to come out of her defeated attitude. A loose case, a broken nose … she needed some encouragement.

"I think it would be someone who has at least *tried* to rock climb in the past but ultimately failed. And not failed like Lutz … but someone who maybe chickened out. And likely not someone with a very social attitude. Someone who is not going to go to someone for help. So probably someone who never really took lessons."

"I like that. But I was thinking more along the lines of someone who *took* lessons, but maybe not for very long. Even if you don't take lessons, you need to at least familiarize yourself with the ropes, the terminology, the safety standards."

"So maybe we start looking around, asking instructors about student that never made it because they froze up."

"Exactly," Mackenzie said. "It makes me wonder how early our friend Lance Tyree wakes up. I think he'd be a reasonable place to start."

"It's only three ten in the morning," Timbrook pointed out.

"So let's give him three hours. In the meantime … you would prefer coffee or a nap?"

"Coffee. But look … anything that happens from here on out, I'm just a tagalong. The docs said I shouldn't do anything strenuous for a couple of days. There were no signs of a concussion, but they want to play it safe."

"No worries. It's not like we'll be climbing mountains or anything."

The joke fell flat, resulting in only a soft chuckle from both of them as Timbrook set off to start a pot of coffee.

Timbrook placed the call to Lance Tyree shortly after six. Because he had already been awake (he was one of those types who woke up ridiculously early to work out), scheduling an early morning meeting with him was easier than either of them had expected. A meeting was arranged at a coffee shop a few blocks away from Tyree's house. On the way, Mackenzie called Ellington—not just to fill him in, but to give him the common courtesy to let him know that her views on the case had changed.

"You do this a lot of the time," he said. "Coming up with some swerve sort of reasoning near the end of a case, usually when most of the people working with you think the case has been closed and taken care of."

"Oh, I know. But how often does it pay off?"

He chuckled and said: "Most of the time. So I take it we're not making our flight?"

"Sorry."

"Hey, this is your show. I just popped up to throw it all off course. What do you need me to do in the meantime?"

"Work with Sheriff Duncan to make sure Brittany Lutz gets a proper psych evaluation. If my hunch is correct, she'll be released for the murder charges by the end of the day...though she'll still be looking at charges for attacking an officer and a federal agent."

"Okay. Keep me posted on this meeting with Tyree."

They ended the call with Mackenzie still getting the sense that he still felt that she had perhaps been unfair to him after he had arrived yesterday. That was a problem for another time, though; they'd have the entire flight back to DC to work on those things.

They met Tyree right on time, sitting down in a corner booth with him at six forty-five. He seemed pleasant enough, apparently not bothered to have been called at such an early hour.

"Was I not enough help before?" he joked as they all settled in.

"That's not the case at all," Timbrook said. "We've got another avenue to look into and were hoping you could push us in the right direction."

"I can certainly try."

"Can you think back to anyone you worked with who only lasted a lesson or two?" Mackenzie asked. "Particularly someone who might have frozen up once they got off of the ground?"

"Well, there are plenty of first-timers who get a few feet off of the ground and go cold. The worst are the ones that are all gung-ho and confident until about one hundred feet or so and then decide it's too much. It's *hell* to get them down."

"I'm looking for someone who might have taken it hard and never come back. Someone you can remember who was visibly upset or frustrated. Anyone like that stand out to you?"

"Actually, yes. A guy named Aaron Pinkett. He's an older guy...sort of well-known around here because he's one of these guys who tries to live off the grid."

"What was your experience with him?"

"He hired me to be his instructor about a year or so ago. That first day we went over the basics. I taught him about ropes, a few basic knots, the sort of equipment he'd need to buy. But, like all of my first-timers, I let them get a taste of climbing to send them home excited. A simple little fifty-foot climb over on the western side of Exum Ridge. It's super simple...a good training place for first-timers. But Aaron got about fifteen feet up and he froze. I mean, he went *rigid*. I had to talk him down. He came down and tried it again, to the same result. I told him we could come back to it later, maybe try some other time. But he said he just couldn't do it."

"That ever happen before with other clients?"

"Sure. A few try it out and decide it's not for them. But the reason Aaron sticks out in my mind is because I saw him a few times after that. I'd be at the park with clients and see him just sitting or standing around popular climb sites just watching people climb."

"Did he ever cause trouble?"

"None that I know of. But I *will* say this...only fifteen or twenty feet up and he was terrified. I've seen people get scared, but he was just out of his mind with fear."

"You said he lives off of the grid. Do you know why?"

"No clue. The little bit of talking he and I did that one lesson, I got the sense that he's just a recluse, you know? He wasn't married, had no real friends to speak of. He said he was interested in climbing just to do something different. When I tried to sort of peel that back, he wasn't big on details. I always like to know *why* people want to start rock climbing. It helps me cater to their personality when I teach them. But Aaron wasn't a big talker. He was probably forty-five or so when we met. Sort of set in his ways already...just wanting to try something new."

"Did you ever try talking to him on any of those times you saw him out and about?" Timbrook asked.

"Once or twice. But he was cold…distant. I just figured he was watching everyone else do something he wasn't able to do, you know?"

The comment sent a chill through Mackenzie as she recalled the bit from Charles Rudeke's audio recording that had set her on this current course.

"Any chance you might know where he lives?" Mackenzie asked.

"I have a rough idea, yeah. Like I said…he's fairly well-known *because* he lives off of the grid. Sort of an in-joke with the locals, poor guy."

"One more thing," Mackenzie said. "When you deal with clients that end up getting scared once they're up there…what percentage end up overcoming that fear and go on to keep climbing?"

"Honestly, I'd say half. Like maybe right down the middle."

"But you're saying Aaron Pinkett was more scared than anyone you'd worked with before?"

"Yeah…so much that he had *me* scared. When I finally got him down…"

"What is it?" Timbrook asked.

"Well, it was almost like he was gone…it was almost like the guy I had worked knots with just fifteen minutes ago had stepped out and someone else had taken his place."

CHAPTER TWENTY NINE

Once again, Mackenzie found herself a passenger in a patrol car, heading down rough secondary roads that wound around the mountains. The directions Tyree had given them to Aaron Pinkett's residence took them in the same direction as Heinz Trail and Devil's Claw, but slight farther south. The roads they traversed went from paved to dirt, then back to paved, and then, at one point, down a back road covered in gravel. Mackenzie assumed that some of the land was owned by Grand Teton National Park, only not actual park grounds, because of the small plots of land that contained mounds of gravel, dirt, and mulch for grounds upkeep. The park was, after all, only a mile or so away from the road they were currently on. The road seemed to border the property line of the park before dipping further away.

Tyree had told them to keep their eyes out for an old black Toyota pickup. Locals had identified it as belonging to Aaron Pinkett, though the cabin he was believed to reside in was about a quarter mile away from where he parked his truck. As Timbrook brought the patrol car around a partially graveled curve, they spotted the black truck just off of the road, parked on what looked like an old cutover of sorts, used for vehicles that had gone too far down these forgotten back roads and needing to turn around.

Timbrook pulled into the small space beside the truck. As Mackenzie got out, she realized that it was a clever place to try hiding a vehicle. They had only spotted it because they were looking for it. Casual passersby would probably not even see it or, at the very least, just catch a fleeting glimpse of it while driving by.

There was an obvious footpath in front of the pull-over spot. It cut through a dense group of trees before the ground bottomed out into a barren little trip of land. There, smaller trees reached skyward, doing very little to hide the slightly overgrown field beyond. Because of the drop-off in the ground and the two different layers of trees, the field could not be seen from the road. And really, there wasn't much of a field to see. It was perhaps thirty yards across and fifty feet in depth. As they walked closer toward it, Mackenzie saw that it wasn't so much a field as a section of land that had been stripped by loggers at some point, given to ruin and overgrown by tall grass and vegetation.

But in the middle of it, there was a small cabin. Actually, to call it a cabin was being generous. It looked more like a shed. It was obvious that it had not seen an ounce of professional construction. The area where the roof met the front wall was covered in places by strips of what looked to be a black tarp. A small weathered picnic table sat to the side, along with a single plastic chair. A good distance away from the little dwelling, there was a hand-crafted fire pit made up of cinderblock fragments and large river rocks. A single pot sat next to one of the rocks, looking like something out of an old westward expansion documentary.

"Son of a bitch," Timbrook said.

"You know this place?"

"No, but we've heard about a guy that lives out in the woods. No complaints, just rumors. We've been getting reports for a year or so but since he never caused problems, we never looked into it."

"No complaints. Sounds promising."

Mackenzie started to step forward but was distracted by a sound behind them. She wasn't certain, but sounded like a car door closing. She turned in that direction, but the copse of trees made it impossible to see the place they had parked.

"You think he's having a visitor?" Timbrook asked.

At that moment, Mackenzie felt her phone vibrate in her pocket. She withdrew it and saw she had a text message. When she read it, she could not decide if she wanted to chuckle or to scream in frustration.

The text read: ***Don't shoot. It's just your husband.***

"What is it?" Timbrook asked.

"Let this be Exhibit A for you. Reasons to maybe not get married."

They stood where they were until about twenty seconds later, they could see Ellington coming through the trees. He looked cautious as he approached, like he knew he had probably pissed Mackenzie off.

"What are you doing here?" she asked him, her tone one of annoyance.

"I know your gut well enough. If you left that early in the morning, I figured you could only be walking into trouble."

"What did you do? Follow us?"

"No. I just tracked you on my phone."

She rubbed her head in the frustration. She wanted to lash out at him; it was a bit embarrassing, especially to appear as if she needed her husband by her side while in front of a woman as capable as Timbrook. On the other hand, maybe his sudden appearance was for the best. If Timbrook had indeed suffered some sort of minor concussion from the blow from Lutz last night, she really had no business being out here. Even if it all turned out to be nothing, there was no sense in her stressing herself out.

"I hate to pull rank here," Mackenzie said, looking at Timbrook. "But I want you to go back to the car. I don't want you risking any further injury. Ellington and I are good from here."

Timbrook looked disappointed and even a bit hurt. But in the end, she nodded her understanding. "Call if anything goes wrong," she said.

Mackenzie nodded, but Timbrook had already turned back toward the woods and the car beyond—perhaps to hide an expression that showed how she truly felt about the situation.

When she was far enough away to be separated from the tension, Mackenzie stepped closer to Ellington. "I'm a little pissed you're here."

"Then why do you look so relieved?"

"Maybe because I regret leaving without waking you up this morning. I was pissed at you then, too."

"I see a pattern here..."

"Yeah, there's a pattern. And we can discuss it later. For now..."

"I know. Waverly filled me in over the phone. He said Timbrook called in to update him. The guy that lives here is a loner, right? Froze up on a few lessons, started sort of obsessing over climbers."

"Something like that. You good to go?"

He only gave a nod and they started walking closer to the little shed-like building. As they got closer, she saw that the door was basically held on with old rusted hinges that had been nailed into an old cracked frame. The place was so run down that she wondered if they were at the right place. Certainly no one could live in such a state—off the grid or not.

As they drew closer to the building, Mackenzie stopped walking. Off to the left and further back, she thought she heard something. Maybe a deer crossing through the forest, maybe just the wind passing through the branches.

But then she heard it again and knew what it was at once. It was hard to tell because of the muted sounds of the forest and the trees to all sides, but it was there. A slight creaking, followed by footfalls.

And it was all coming from behind the little shed-like structure.

"He's on the move," Mackenzie said.

She took off at a run to the right side of the building. Ellington did the same, angling in front of her. There was a moment where her heart thrummed, once again back in action with Ellington at her side. But the potential danger in the situation made that warm feeling fade very quickly.

Whether he realized it or not, Ellington took the lead as he cut in front of her. He was drawing his gun and ran close along the outer wall for cover. Mackenzie barely had time to be irritated by this, though. As they neared the back corner of the dwelling, she heard a *thump* and then a muffed grunt from Ellington.

As Mackenzie came around the side of the building, she saw a man standing at the corner. He was holding a wooden baseball bat and leering down at Ellington, who was on his hands and knees trying to scramble back to his feet, gasping for air on the ground. The man was raising the bat over his head, preparing to strike Ellington while he was down.

"Drop it!" Mackenzie yelled as she drew the Glock from her holster. The man redirected his gaze toward her and instead of bringing the bat down in a lethal blow to Ellington's head, he threw it forward instead. It came, wobbling end over end, directly at Mackenzie's face. She had a spit second to decide: shoot at the man or stop the bat from crushing her face in.

She held her hands up, the bat striking the underside of her right arm. A flaring pins and needles sensation went spiraling up her arm as the bat rebound and struck the ground.

She uttered a curse and tried to shake the feeling back into her arm as the man took off at a mad dash toward the woods behind the cabin.

Mackenzie stepped forward and knelt down to Ellington.. Thankfully, the blow had not struck his head or face. He was doubled over in pain, holding his stomach and gasping.

"What did he hit?" she asked.

"Stomach. Rib...maybe. Damn..."

Mackenzie looked to the tree line behind the shed. The attacker—presumably Aaron Pinkett—had already made it into the trees. She looked back to Ellington and frowned. "I'm going after him."

"Mac..."

She kissed him on the cheek and got to her feet. She took another five seconds to pull out her phone. She pulled up Timbrook's number and the moment she answered the phone, Mackenzie cut her off before she could even say hello.

"Ellington is down, Pinkett is on the run. Call in assistance and then come help Ellington, please."

She hung up before Timbrook could utter so much as a word. She looked back to Ellington one last time before heading toward the tree line.

"Mac!" Ellington's voice was strained and urgent.

"What?" she hissed at him, sensing precious seconds slipping away while Pinkett was escaping into the woods.

"Sorry," he grunted. "I love you."

"I love you, too," she said, not realizing just how much she meant it until the words were out of her mouth.

She then turned back toward the trees and took off after Pinkett, her borrowed sidearm drawn and her feet anxious for the chase.

CHAPTER THIRTY

If Aaron Pinkett was indeed responsible for the three climber deaths, he was not doing much in the way of remaining inconspicuous. He made absolutely no attempt to quietly escape. He was barreling through the forest, making it quite easy for Mackenzie to follow after him. The only obstacle was that he was far enough ahead of her to be out of sight; she was having to rely on sound alone to track him. She had to stop after every few strides to make sure she was headed in the right direction.

She had been running no more than thirty seconds when she realized that it might have been foolish to go running after him. Pinkett knew these woods much better than she did. This became eerily evident when she started to see small footpaths breaking away to either side of the route she was currently on.

This told her several things, none of which made her feel especially confident. First, it was evidence that he did indeed know these forests well—so well that he had a tiny network of footpaths behind his ramshackle home. It also made her wonder just where these trails went. She recalled the trail where they had discovered Tim Wyatt's little love shack.

If a killer had access to this secret network of trails, they could have easy access to any climbing spots in the area. More than that, they would also have convenient escape routes to get away from the scene as quickly as possible.

Mackenzie came to another stop, cocking her head to listen for the sound of Pinkett's progress through the forest. Again, she located him easily, down one of the trails that forked off in front of her, hard to the left.

As she followed him, she noticed that the ground was starting to rise up slightly. This close to the mountains and cliffs out at Grand Teton, she supposed it made sense. But once again, it made her feel as if she were walking directly into some sort of planned-out trap. And with every panicked stride he took away from her, the more confident she became that he was guilty of *something*—even if it was only hammering a federal agent with a baseball bat.

The path she was on forked off again after another thirty seconds or so, but she could easily hear Pinkett clambering through the trees ahead. The incline to the ground grew a bit more severe, but he seemed to be having no trouble keeping pace and outrunning her. It probably also helped that he knew the terrain much better than she did.

The trail bore to the right, the incline getting a bit harsher. Mackenzie was having to hunch over, using her hands to grab outcropped roots to help her along. She stopped for a moment to make sure she could still hear Pinkett's progress through the forest.

There was nothing…just a bird trilling somewhere nearby. But in terms of footfalls or snapping twigs and low-hanging branches, there was nothing.

Mackenzie gripped the handle of the Glock, assuming he was hiding somewhere. Waiting to strike, waiting to take her out. God only knew what he had hiding out here.

But then she craned her neck up to see what was waiting further ahead. The footpath meandered further up a bit and then leveled off as it cut to the left. There, the trail came to a stop. So did the forest, though it was hard to tell why from where she stood. But as she glanced up, it made sense—and it also made her feel small.

The trail stopped in front of a tall granite wall. It was gray and black, mostly shadowed by the trees along its side from where she stood. She couldn't tell how far up it went—her angle from the inclined ground made it impossible to tell—but there was one thing she knew for certain.

Pinkett was scaling the wall. She could see a slight blur through the trees, going up the wall. He was moving at a surprising speed, making Mackenzie assume he knew the holds and crevices along that wall just as well as he knew the trails he had just led her down.

For only a single moment, she thought about rushing back to the little building Pinkett called a home. She could give coordinates to the police and someone could probably figure out where this wall led to—probably to level ground that led to a more towering wall or mountain face if she had to guess. Again, from her vantage point, it was impossible to tell.

But Mackenzie had never been a fan of *probably*.

She continued up the trail, her calves burning again. But it was starting to feel familiar—it was starting to feel good. By the time she neared the top of the hill, she felt almost back to normal, back to the Mackenzie White shape before she'd gotten pregnant.

She glanced up to the rock wall and saw that Pinkett was much further up than she had expected. Twenty-five, maybe thirty feet already.

She aimed her gun up and took aim. She had a clean shot. She could take him anywhere she wanted. But she also knew that if he fell from that height, there was a chance he could break his neck or back and die. And if he was the killer they had been looking for, it was always better to have them alive and able to share their insights and, God forbid, other victims no one knew about.

"Pinkett, stop where you are," she yelled. "I've got a clean shot. You keep climbing, I'll take it."

He did not stop. He did not even look down. He was calling her bluff. Apparently, he was thinking the same thing she was: he was better to her alive rather than smeared on the ground.

"Shit," Mackenzie said.

She approached the wall and looked up. It was quite rough and rugged—the sort that provided plenty of handholds and footrests. But as she reached up for the first grip, she saw the real reason why. There were climber bolts embedded into the wall, easy handholds located at strategic locations in the wall to make the climb easier.

Apparently, Pinkett had been practicing on this wall—and had gotten quite good. He was climbing in a way that indicated he basically had the holds and bolts down to a science.

If he was indeed the killer and was struggling with some sort of fear of heights or climbing, she figured this would be a good place to try to quash them. The same route, over and over again, would work wonders.

Mackenzie readied herself, grabbed the first natural handhold, and propelled herself up to grip onto the first installed bolt. Her feet scrambled for purchase and when her right one found a thin little ridge, she panted her toes and pushed herself up to allow her left arm to stretch out and up to the next bolt. It was a little out of her reach, but a yoga-like stretch allowed her to grab it.

She pressed her body against the wall and looked up. Pinkett was well ahead of her, but she was ignoring him for the moment. If she was really going to do this, she was going to have to put everything into it. She studied the bolts; they were easy enough to see, little silver glints protruding from the side of the rock face. From her perspective, they looked like nothing more than little nails, but she knew that they were all roughly the size of a closed fist.

She started to reach up for the next one—slightly to her right—when the memory of her long-ago instructor surfaced.

"You'll have to come down on your own and get help..."

The blood... the certainty that he was going to die and that it was her fault...

She shook her head defiantly. Nope... not today. She discarded the thought and the memory as she reached up for the next bolt. She pulled herself up, placed her foot on the bolt her hand had just been, and continued to climb upward.

Pinkett was taking notice now. He was at least thirty feet above her but had finally stopped to pay her some attention. When she had been on the ground, he seemed not to care much about her once he made it to the wall. But he seemed hesitant now. She watched as he looked from her and then back down to the ground before starting back up the wall.

Mackenzie followed after him, doing her very best not to look down. Instead, she looked up, trying to determine where, exactly, this wall ended. She had seen no immediate mountains directly behind Pinkett's little campsite and knew that their chase through the woods had been little more than a mile or so. She was quite sure this was not an actual mountain face of any kind, but could easily be the lead-up to a much more severe climb.

But she couldn't worry about that. Not yet, anyway. For now, she had to make up time—to try to catch up to Pinkett before he reached the top.

She could hear Pinkett from above her. He seemed to be chuckling a bit, laughing nervously and speaking to himself. "You're doing it," he told himself. "You're actually doing it because you *have* *to* do it." More of that strange laughter followed this.

This unsettled Mackenzie a bit but she climbed on, undeterred.

She was fortunate that it had not rained recently. It allowed her a dry grip on each bolt, though she did have to press her hand against the rock every now and then to remove some of the sweat from her palms. She didn't really have the convenience of climbing gloves or chalk to assist with her climb.

She was also fortunate that Pinkett was apparently not very confident in his climbing abilities. The bolts were placed in a way that might be featured on an indoor climbing wall for beginners. There were a few places where they were spaced apart in such a way that made her think he might have been trying to challenge himself, but it was easy going for the most part.

She focused on climbing, on switching hands and giving attention to the muscles in her fingers. Her toes were getting a bit sore from placing weight on the bolts and pushing upward, but it wasn't too bad for right now. She climbed, hand over hand, scaling the wall and refusing to look down. She felt that new memory still trying to steal the show, trying to sabotage her, but she pushed it as far back as she could. She did so by hyper-focusing on the climb, on each and every movement of her body—reinforcing it with the reminder that she had no ropes or safety of any kind.

If she fell, she was likely dead.

She glanced up again and saw that she was indeed gaining on him. But she could also see the end of the wall. It came to a ragged stop roughly fifteen feet over Pinkett's head. Realizing this, Mackenzie couldn't help herself; she looked down.

The world swam for a moment. She knew she had been climbing fast, but had lost track of time. She figured she had been climbing for perhaps five minutes. Maybe a bit more. But she had not been expecting this.

It was hard to properly gauge from being pressed against the wall, but she guessed she was eighty feet in the air. Probably not quite one hundred feet yet, but close.

Her arms started to tremble at the reality of this. She could feel her heart pumping erratically as fear flooded it. She looked back up one more time and saw that Pinkett's own movements were slow as well. She estimated that the distance from the very bottom to the top that Pinkett was nearing was somewhere around one hundred and twenty feet.

She took a deep breath and pushed on. The fear could have been crippling, but she didn't give it room to grow. She kept forging on, from one bolt to the next. Her jaw was clenched and her muscles tightened, as if trying to convince her heart that she had this—that there was no way in hell they were not making it to the top.

That's when she looked up and saw that Pinkett was at the top. He was pulling himself up, the top portion of his body hidden by the summit as his legs kicked at the air.

Anger flared up, momentarily replacing the fear. Mackenzie climbed on with laser focus. She was so intent on getting to the top that she missed one of the bolts as she reached out for it. Her arm fell forward, dangling in the air for a moment. She clutched the bolt she was holding onto it with her left hand, making sure she retained her balance instead of waving uncontrollably and loosening her grip. It was harder that it would have been if she'd had all of her core strength, but her abs had gone to hell ever since the pregnancy.

She steadied herself and tried to find the balance between hurrying and making sure she didn't fall to her death. She had to be aware of each movement, trying to ignore that she was suspended in the air, clinging to a rock wall where one incorrect motion could kill her. It was easy enough, one hand moving and then the next. She did it with such ease during some transitions that it made her wonder how she had so easily given up on it much earlier in her life.

She could do this. She could make it to the top and then she assumed the chase would continue. And if she ever got her hands on Pinkett—

That thought crashed to the bottom of her mind when she heard something clattering beside her. A piece of the rock wall and come loose and fallen. She watched it fall down, shrinking as it went, reminding her how high up she was.

For a sick moment, she felt gravity like an actually physical presence. And it was trying to pull her off of the wall.

She reached for the next bolt and heard that clattering again— rock striking rock multiple times. But it was coming from overhead.

She peered up, craning her neck, and saw what was really going on. Pinkett stood at the edge of the summit. He held something in his hands as he leered down at her. She was pretty sure it was a collection of sizeable rocks.

Shit...

As she watched, he threw another one down. And this one looked like it had the proper aim. Mackenzie could only watch hopelessly as the rock rushed down toward her, growing larger by the second.

CHAPTER THIRTY ONE

The rock struck her between the neck and her right shoulder, just above her breast. Had it struck her about an inch or two higher, it would have probably shattered her collarbone. It made a meaty sound as it rebounded from her and continued on its way to the ground.

A shock of pain flared through her and her muscles reacted as they normally would. Her right hand released the bolt it was clutching. And as part of the shock, the rest of her body responded in kind. Her right knee buckled, causing her foot to slip away from the bolt it was standing on. When the right side of her body faltered, her left side overcompensated for balance. Her legs were both dangling in the air, her full weight held by only her left hand.

She could feel her grip weakening, the muscles in her palm and fingers trembling. The pain below her right shoulder was tremendous but the adrenaline rushing through her muted it enough for her to stretch it up in order to regain the bolt she'd been holding. She wasted no time, right away going for the next one.

She looked up and saw that Pinkett was still there. He had another rock in his hand and threw it down hard. She could tell right away that it was going to miss—though not by much. It went sailing by her left arm by no more than a foot. She went to the next bolt, then the next, taking less than five seconds to clear them.

She knew this made her an easier target for Pinkett, but she was okay with that. She steadied herself, unmoving as she clung to the bolts in a strange X-shape along the wall. She peered up and slowly started to lower her right arm. Her left hand was starting to ache from the climbing, but she currently trusted it to support her weight than her right arm which was starting to tingle from the blow she'd taken moments ago. Besides... she had other plans for her right hand for the moment.

She waited for Pinkett to draw back with the next rock. There were less than twenty feet between them now—probably closer to fifteen. She could see the rock in his hand as he hefted it up. It was the size of a softball; if it struck her in the head, it might kill her before the impact below would.

As he held it up, prepared to bring it down, Mackenzie acted as quickly as she could, not wanting to giver herself away. She drew the Glock carefully, nearly dragging it along the rock wall—which would have slowed her progress and likely affected her left-handed grip. But her movement was fluid and when she aimed and pulled the trigger all at once, she had to arch her back the slightest bit.

When she got the shot off, there was a paralyzing moment where she thought she had released the side of the wall. A cry rose up in her throat, as she was sure she was falling.

But she hugged the wall, dropping the Glock in the process. She heard the clattering noise as it bounced down the wall. She also heard the plinks and clacks of Pinkett's projectile again as the rock intended for her bounced down the wall several feet away. She took a deep breath, steadied her nerves, and glanced up.

Aaron Pinkett was nowhere to be seen.

Not wanting to waste a second, Mackenzie started climbing again. Her muscles were on fire and there was a fear in her stomach like she had never felt before. She had nearly died far too many times in the last minute or so and it felt like she was on adrenaline overload. She took the last few bolts to the summit like a mad-woman. She was so spiked with adrenaline that she had to blot her sweaty hands against the rock wall after every bolt but she still made it to the top quickly.

She was partially expecting Pinkett to be right there at the edge, waiting for her. After all, wasn't that what he had been doing?

Wasn't that how he had killed the climbers so far? Waiting for them finish their climb?

As her hands reached up for the solid ground at the summit, she was expecting him to stamp on her hands of kick her in the face. But she pulled herself up off of the wall, sliding onto the rocky ground at the top. She let out a strangled little moan, swallowing down what she felt might be a legitimate freak-out. She made it; she was alive. But it wasn't until now, at the end of it, that she realized the amount of jeopardy she had been in.

Had things gone even the slightest bit different, she would have left Kevin in this world without a mother.

She scrambled to her knees, struggling to find her feet. She realized then just how much the climb had taken out of her. If her shot had missed Pinkett, there was no telling how far away he was. And if he had a head start, he'd never catch her.

She looked ahead and saw a small jutting area of rock, about ten feet wide and fifteen feet long. Beyond that, there were tall weeds and encroaching trees. Behind those trees, another rock wall began. This one was much higher than the one she had just scaled and, a bit further up, connected with an even larger rock wall to make up a small mountain.

But her eyes were drawn away from the mountain. She looked to the tall grass, where something was moving. It was a hunched shape, barely having made it into the grass. Mackenzie walked in that direction, beyond relieved to be putting distance between herself and the rock wall she had just conquered.

After taking three steps across the rock rocky ground, she saw the blood. There wasn't much, but just enough to make a trail to follow. It led her to the grass, some of which came up to her waist. There was more blood on the grass and it looked to be a larger amount. As she made her way deeper into the tall grass, she noticed another of those footpaths that had flattened a thin portion of the weeds. It was headed straight and bearing to the right.

She reached for the Glock that was no longer there and then balled her hands into fists—which made her right shoulder feel as if someone had set it on fire.

The shape moving through the grass was Pinkett. He was about ten feet in front of her, trying to get to his feet but unable to do so. He scooted forward on his knees as he made a strange choking sound.

Mackenzie closed the distance between them. She knelt down next to him, stopped him from making his way through the grass, and pushed him over.

Her bullet had taken him in high in the chest, slightly left of center. Another two inches and it would have erased the left side of his throat. As it was, the wound was spouting blood. It was hard to tell if he was going to make it.

He had a dazed, otherworldly look in his eyes, a look she had seen many times—the look of someone fighting for life, someone between two worlds. He spotted her and actually smiled.

"I did it," he said softly, almost sad. "I made it up…"

She thought back on all the suffering he had caused, and more than anything she wanted to let him die.

She paused for a moment, considering it.

But only for a moment. She could not let him die. Whether he deserved it or not, it was not the humane thing to do.

Mackenzie tore at the grass around her, making a heaping handful of it. She wadded it up and then pressed it against Pinkett's wound.

He struggled against her, writhing. But again, he smiled and repeated: "I did it. I really did it. Ha!"

He struggled against her though, as if he did not want her help. Ironic, she realized. Fighting with this man to save his life.

Finally, he was too weak to fight anymore. He gave up, and let her staunch it.

He lay there, staring up to the sky and the mountain ahead of them, letting out a series of wet breaths.

His gaze fell upon her. He stared into her eyes, and it was like staring into the very soul of evil. It was a look, she knew, that would haunt her forever.

She forced herself to look away as she took out her phone and prepared to call for help.

Finally, the nightmare was over.

CHAPTER THIRTY TWO

Kevin was screaming and, quite frankly, it was like music to Mackenzie's ears.

It was time for his nighttime bottle—the one he seemed to be the most impatient for. But he was down to only one feeding a night, so Mackenzie was not going to complain. She got out of bed, placing a gentle hand on Ellington's arm as she felt him trying to edge out of bed.

"Don't even think about it," she said. "I've got him."

He only grunted. He'd suffered three broken ribs from Pinkett's blow with the baseball bat. His doctors were making him sleep in a slightly elevated sleeping position, which he hated. Given the way their last day in Wyoming had played out, she was well aware that she was fortunate to have come away with nothing more than a massive bruise on the right side of her chest.

She crept into Kevin's room and picked him up. It took some effort to get him comfortable on her left side, but he seemed content enough as she gave him his bottle. She sat down in the rocking chair with him, rocking in the darkness. She closed her eyes and took it all in, well aware that two days ago, she had come just a few fingers from never seeing him again.

She had assumed that once she and Ellington got home, there would be a lot to adjust to: the strange tension between them and Ellington's choice to join her while leaving Kevin with his mother, Mackenzie's recently resurfaced memories, Ellington's broken ribs. But none of that had come up yet. So far, there was an unspoken peace between them, a gratitude fueled by the fact that they were all back together, the three of them, a family.

Mackenzie was surprised—startled, really—to find that all of her time and energy had not gone directly to dissecting the memory of her younger self on that rock wall, her wounded instructor below. No, instead, her thoughts had been centered on Aaron Pinkett. He had still been alive when help had arrived in the form of a Jeep about half a mile from where she had done her best to keep him alive. As far as she knew, he had been alive—albeit in critical condition in the hospital—when she and Ellington had caught their plane back home.

Bur she kept seeing that faraway look in his eyes as death had tried to creep in. He'd looked like a normal man, though she supposed everyone did when they were that close to death. And as she had done her best to keep him from bleeding out, she had also had to wrestle with the fact that they had not known, to that point, if he was even the killer.

There was enough evidence in his little shack to assume that he was. There were bits and pieces of climber detritus from other climbers, as if he had been making a collection: discarded strands of rope, rusted carabiners, even an old discarded shoe. They'd also found an old Moleskine notebook that served as a journal of sorts—notes that proved Mackenzie's theory correct.

Pinkett had lived in shame of his fear of heights. He had grown into adulthood not *envying* those without the phobia, but *hating* them. It was a rage that he decided to carry out in grisly ways. Mackenzie had not stuck around to read all of the entries in the notebook, but she did see where Pinkett had specifically named Mandy Yorke and Charles Rudeke in his rantings.

She shook the thoughts away as she heard the familiar sucking noises that signified that Kevin's bottle was empty. She looked down and saw that he was fading fast again, his belly full and his cheeks dimpled with a tiny smile. She held him a while longer, as if trying to burn the feel of it into her memory.

That way, perhaps deciding to take a case or not take a case would not be such a dilemma in the future. She kissed the top of his head as she placed him back into the crib and then walked to back to her bedroom.

Ellington was still awake, sighing heavily as she reclaimed her place beside him.

"Still hurting?" she asked.

"It's actually not so bad right now. I was just thinking about how stupid I was to come out there. I was selfish … and certainly not putting Kevin first."

"True. But if you hadn't come, Timbrook would have been with me when we chased Pinkett behind his house. She was already hurt. That blow could have really put her out."

"Is that the glass-half-full approach?"

"It's an I'm-glad-the-glass-isn't-broken approach."

She leaned over and kissed him softly on the mouth before she put her head on her pillow. As she drifted off to sleep, she again thought of that look on Pinkett's fading face and prayed it would not follow her into her dreams.

When the FaceTime tone sounded out from her phone, Mackenzie was doing her best to fold one of Kevin's onesies—something she had still not quite gotten the hang of. It was Sunday, five days after she and Ellington had arrived back home from Wyoming. She was expecting McGrath to touch base any day now, but he never FaceTimed.

She grabbed up her phone and was delighted to see Timbrook's name on the display. She accepted it and smiled as Sergeant Timbrook's face filled the screen. She looked much happier than she had for most of Mackenzie's visit to Jackson Hole.

"Good morning, Sergeant," she said.

"Hi, Agent White. Sorry to bother you on a Sunday…"

"You're not bothering me," Mackenzie said, and meant it. She could hear Ellington somewhere in the apartment behind her, talking in his too-cute baby voice to Kevin. It made her heart happy—made her feel like today was going to be an amazing day.

"I was mainly just calling because I thought you might want an update. The doctors have officially given Pinkett a positive diagnosis. Something went wrong two days ago and there was a blood transfusion involved, but he's mostly recovered. They expect him to be discharged sometime in the next few days."

"Were you able to find anything else to help convict him?"

"We did, actually. In turns out that some of the discarded rope we found in his shack once belonged to Mandy Yorke. But even beyond that...he gave a full confession last night."

"What?"

Timbrook nodded. "Yeah. He broke down...right after the doctors told him how close he had come to dying—how lucky he was. He just broke. He admitted to all of it. He smashed Bryce Evans's head in with a hammer before Evans fell. He cut Mandy Yorke's line as she was climbing Exum Ridge, right as she neared the summit. And with Charles Rudeke, he was waiting at the top of Devil's Claw and just pushed him."

"Did he explain why?"

"He did, but it seems like gibberish. He did admit to being angry, being absolutely overwhelmed with fear when it came to heights. Said this was his way of processing through it, of, and I'm quoting here, getting rid of the demon of fear. Said he had nothing against the people he killed...just that he envied them enough to kill them. If he couldn't do it, why should they? That sort of thing."

"My God."

"Anyway...you were such a huge help, I thought you'd want to know."

"Absolutely. Thank you. And hey...Timbrook. Don't be a stranger. Check in with me from time to time, would you?"

The suggestion seemed to both surprise and delight Timbrook. She smiled and said, "Sure. I can do that. Thanks, Agent White."

They ended the call and Mackenzie turned toward the sound of Kevin cooing. Ellington was bringing him into the living room, the two smiling at one another as Kevin grabbed Ellington's nose and gave it a squeeze.

"Was that Timbrook?" Ellington asked, his voice a bit cut off from his nose being held hostage.

"Yeah."

"Any new information on the case?"

She nearly told him all of it, glad to know that she had been able to help bring Aaron Pinkett to justice. But she looked at them both—the boys in her life—and the need to focus on the success of the case faded. She smiled, her heart turning happily in her chest.

"Not right now," she said. "Maybe later."

"You okay?" Ellington asked.

Mackenzie smiled, walked across the room, and wrapped her arms around Ellington. She kissed him softly on the mouth. Kevin squirmed between them and she placed a kiss on top of his head.

"Yes," Mackenzie said. "I'm great."

And God, did it feel good to say that and actually mean it.

Now Available for Pre-Order!

BEFORE HE STALKS
(A Mackenzie White Mystery—Book 13)

From Blake Pierce, bestselling author of ONCE GONE (a #1 best-seller with over 900 five star reviews), comes book #13 in the heart-pounding Mackenzie White mystery series.

When bodies are found dead on the rainy shores of Puget Sound and there are no leads in sight, FBI Special Agent Mackenzie White is assigned the case. Believing this to be run-of-the-mill homicides that will let her ease back into the field, Mackenzie soon realizes she's in for more than she bargained for.

Racing against time and a gruesome body count, Mackenzie finds herself delving into the mind of a psychotic serial killer, caught in a game of cat and mouse. As she struggles to come back to work after just giving birth, she wonders if this may be too much for her to handle.

And when things can't get any worse, there comes a shocking twist that even she can't predict.

A dark psychological thriller with heart-pounding suspense, BEFORE HE STALKS is book #13 in a riveting new series—with a beloved new character—that will leave you turning pages late into the night.

Also available by Blake Pierce is ONCE GONE (A Riley Paige mystery—Book #1), a #1 bestseller with over 1,200 five star reviews—and a free download!

BEFORE HE STALKS
(A Mackenzie White Mystery—Book 13)

Did you know that I've written multiple novels in the mystery genre? If you haven't read all my series, click the image below to download a series starter!